QUEEN OF FATE & FIRE

Rogue Ethereal Book Six

ANNIE ANDERSON

QUEEN of FATE & FIRE
Rogue Ethereal Book 6
International Bestselling Author
Annie Anderson

Edited by Angela Sanders
Cover Design by Danielle Fine

www.annieande.com
Official Annie Anderson Newsletter

For those that have been found.

"She was soft as an angel but oh, she could love with the fury of a demon."

— N.R. HART

BOOKS BY ANNIE ANDERSON

GRAVE TALKER SERIES

Dead to Me

SOUL READER SERIES

Night Watch

ROGUE ETHEREAL SERIES

Woman of Blood & Bone

Daughter of Souls & Silence

Lady of Madness & Moonlight

Sister of Embers & Echoes

Priestess of Storms & Stone

Queen of Fate & Fire

PHOENIX RISING SERIES

Flame Kissed

Death Kissed

Fate Kissed

Shade Kissed

Sight Kissed

SHELTER ME SERIES

Seeking Sanctuary

Reaching Refuge

Chasing Cover

Seek You Find Me

(A Romantic Suspense Newsletter Serial)

CHAPTER ONE

They say the first year of marriage was the hardest. If the blade to my new husband's throat was any indication, they—whoever *they* were—would be right.

But this wasn't my husband—not really.

Sure, this was Alistair's body, and sure, he was probably hidden somewhere, crouched low in the recesses of his own mind, but the man looking through Alistair's eyes, and wearing Alistair's skin was not my husband. He was some kind of dark Fae, and he'd taken over.

"What have you done with him? Where is he?" I'd meant it to come out as commanding, but I didn't quite hit the mark. I was a frantic mess at best, and the monster wearing my husband's skin knew it.

This was what I got for coming to Faerie. Literally

every single person with any lick of sense said demons could get possessed here. They said it was too risky. They said Alistair was in danger by following me to this place.

Did I listen?

Of course not. I smiled, nodded, and did whatever the fuck I wanted to anyway, and look where we were. Look at what happened to the man I loved.

I should have known something was off the moment I saw Alistair fall in the gorge. We'd been trying to keep the Unseelie Fae back. We were trying to stop Verena and whatever cracked plot she was trying to carry out. I'd thought we'd succeeded. Peering into the strikingly blue eyes of Alistair's hijacked face, I'd say we missed one.

I saw the lie cross his face before he opened his mouth. *No. Not today, buddy.*

"Think very carefully about what you say next." I could practically feel my molars cracking from how hard I was clenching my jaw, and if my blade happened to nick his neck, well, it was just a sign that I meant business.

And yeah, this was far too close to home for me. Not just that it was Alistair—not that it was the man I loved being used in such a fashion. No, this was Maria all over again. This was everything I'd buried bubbling up to the surface.

And if Alistair's face wavered a little due to some unshed tears, well, I'd say I'd earned them.

Not-Alistair took that moment to pounce, bringing the sword from his scabbard up and knocking my blade away from his neck.

I scrambled back a step, before our swords clashed—or rather my athame went from dagger-sized to short-sword sized after I pressed the rune on the handle, and I attacked. My fencing skills were weak at best, but no-rules swordplay? Aidan had once said I was a natural.

Still, this guy was parrying every single strike like he was humoring me rather than fighting for his life.

"I am not your enemy," Not-Alistair's mouth said, but his voice was no longer my husband's. It had a burr of something else I couldn't place. A smokiness that had never been there before—not even when he'd been phased.

"Really? You got a funny way of showing it." My frustration bubbled up inside my chest as I slashed and parried. I couldn't say why I didn't want to use the power that roiled beneath my skin, but I didn't.

I could kill him. I could hurt him. But I didn't want to because of the face he wore. It was a weakness I knew I had, but I didn't have the luxury of time to analyze it.

"I didn't want to take over this body," he grunted, staving off the edge of my blade with a bit less finesse than before. "It was the only way I could talk to you. I tried in the valley. But you couldn't understand me. I helped you, remember? I am on your side."

I had a tough time remembering the battle. Everything from the last twenty-four hours was a blur of one shit-show after another.

"I tossed Verena into a cliff face like she was—what do humans call it? A frisbee?" he offered, not unkindly.

That rang a bell. A huge monster of a Fae had taken Verena out for us, and then helped us fight the rest of the zombie-looking Fae back to the door. "Smoke guy?"

All the while, our blades were spinning as we slashed and parried and stabbed at one another—or rather I did the stabbing and slashing, and Not-Alistair, AKA, Smoke Guy parried and danced around me. Granted, I was wearing him down, but he still hadn't had so much as another nick from my steel. Or whatever the hell these blades were made of.

"Niall, little goddess. My name is Niall."

I found I liked the use of the goddess title no better than "highness" or "majesty" and growled at him. "I don't care who you are. Give me back my husband. *Now*."

If he even could. I couldn't get Maria back. Who was to say I could get Alistair? Who was to say that this would be how everyone left me? My nose began to sting, and his face wobbled and distorted.

"I will. I have no intention of staying in this body. I will return him to you alive, intact, and unharmed. I promise. I just need your help."

For some reason, even though his words made sense and his tone was kind, I brought my sword down harder, my slashes sped up, my jabs grew sharper. He was lying. Alistair had been taken away from me just like she had.

"I don't believe you." With that, I shoved at him with my mind, causing his body to fly back into the wall as my blade kissed his throat.

I didn't even hear the footsteps behind me before my mother started speaking. "You know, I'm all for setting my husband's head on fire, but I've never actually tried cutting it off. You think that would work, or is that just a good way to become a widow?"

I couldn't help it, I snorted, a sharp bark of laughter bubbling up my throat. Still, I didn't move my gaze even a millimeter from Alistair's stolen ones.

"This isn't Alistair." Yes, I knew I probably looked like I'd cracked. Here I was holding a sword to my husband's throat insisting that he wasn't my husband.

Like a crazy person.

Which totally explained why Teresa was shifting her weight from foot to foot as she tried to decide what to do next. "It's his body, but it's not him. Remember how everyone said demons could be infected by Fae? Meet Niall, Mom."

The heat of fire blooming in my mother's hand swept over me, and I relaxed just a smidgen. She didn't think I was crazy.

"Like I told your daughter, I need your help. This was the only way I could speak to you. Please. I don't want to quarrel with you or yours, and I will give this body back unharmed. Just listen to me. Please. The fate of Faerie depends on it."

It didn't matter how much I wanted to believe him, I didn't know if I could. I didn't know if I could trust Niall.

"Go on," my mother prompted. "If you say the fate of Faerie depends on you delivering a message, give it to us and then return Alistair."

Niall's lips—so different than any expression Alistair had ever shown me—twisted in indignation. "You won't listen. You won't do what I need you to. My only leverage is this body. Faerie and all Fae will die if you don't. I can't risk it." He shook his head like he was coming to a decision. "I will not leave this body until the task is done."

"Sure. I'll just drop everything and let an Unseelie Fae lead me on an epic quest. Who the fuck do you think you are? Give him back to me, or so help me, I'll kill him to save him from you."

Niall shook his head, his pitying expression pissing me the fuck off. "No, you won't. You love this man too much. It is a harsh thing I do, Little Goddess, but it is what I must. I pray you might forgive me one day, doing this horrible thing to you. But maybe not. Stealing him away—even for such a short time—is cruel, I know. I do not wish to do it. But there are many things I have done in service to your family that I had never wished for. Still, these things must be done."

None of this smelled like a lie. It didn't mean any of it made sense or was the truth, either. The Fae were a tricky lot, and they could lie without trying. Still.

I couldn't help asking a question that had been on my mind throughout all of this. "Is he okay? Is he hurt?"

"No, child. He is safe. Right brassed off at me for stealing his body, but he is safe inside his mind."

I couldn't say why that gave me a bit of relief, but it did. "So he can see me? Hear me?"

Niall nodded before pinching my blade between his thumb and pointer finger and gently pushing it back. He did this with enough power that I knew there was no way I could have bested him in a sword fight—or any other fight for that matter.

"I am not here to hurt you. I am not here to injure you or yours in any way. Please listen. Please. We don't have much time."

"Tell me what he's saying to you," I ordered. "Tell me what he's saying, and I'll listen. I'll believe you that he's okay in there. I'll let you speak."

Niall considered me for a second before his eyes went unfocused. He looked like he was listening to a far-off voice. "To the ends of the earth and far beyond. Vaster than Heaven or Hell or any of the worlds in between."

I couldn't help it, I started crying in earnest, relief making me wilt to the stone floor. Those were the words Alistair had said when he told me he loved me. He was in there. He was.

When I'd gotten myself marginally under control, I touched the rune on my athame, collapsing the blade into a dagger and sheathed it.

"I'll listen. I can't promise to do what you need, but I will listen."

Niall considered me, a faint trace of approval in his half-smile. "I appreciate a goddess who doesn't make promises she doesn't think she can keep. You remind me of your father."

"Lying pisses me off. What can I say?" I shrugged before indelicately wiping my eyes and nose. "You knew Dušan?"

"No, child. I *know* Dušan. And we need him back before this world and everyone made from it collapses into nothing."

I couldn't help the half-crazed bark of laughter that bubbled up from my throat. I sounded like I needed a straitjacket STAT. "Well, that's tough shit, Niall.

Dušan is dead. Has been for about four hundred years."

I kept giggling as I turned to my mother. "I guess we're fucked then, huh?"

I personally felt I had every right to crack. I mean, hadn't I stopped one Apocalypse after the other? Hadn't I lost enough? Sure. Let's add in an entire realm of people and my life while we were at it. Absolutely. That would be the cherry on top.

So, there I was—giggling like a loon as I sat splayed on the floor of a Faerie castle that I was now the apparent Queen of, and my husband was possessed by a dark Fae.

Someone just shoot me now.

Niall crouched at my feet, concern etched in Alistair's face. "I don't know where you heard Dušan was dead, but I can assure you, he is not. For one, we're all alive. If he were dead, this realm would have collapsed in on itself. Secondly, I have no idea where you got the idea that gods were so easily killed, but one little changeling who is more human than anything else does not have the power to murder a god—especially not the father of all gods."

I supposed Niall could be right. Dušan was in a little pocket of existence he'd made for himself, so I assumed it was possible that he could be alive. How I thought I could possibly convince a god older than time that he was wrong was anyone's guess.

"Again, child, we don't have time. If we do not get Dušan back before the Blood Moon rises, this realm will be lost."

I snorted, rolling my eyes. *Blood Moon.* How fucking cliché. "Fine. How much time do we have until this *Blood Moon?*"

"Three days."

Yeah, I started giggling again, but could anyone blame me? I had three days to get my birth father back from the brink of existence.

Piece of cake.

CHAPTER TWO

After I stopped giggling—which probably took far too long considering my current time constraint—I did what any rational person would do when given a task far too big to tackle. I conjured myself some top-shelf bourbon and drank that shit right out of the bottle.

Okay, so a more rational person would probably brainstorm ways to complete said impossible task, but I was tapped out on brainstorming sessions for the time being. Once I was sure I wasn't dreaming, nor could I find a logical reason not to believe the ancient dark Fae trapped in my husband's body, I handed the bottle off to my mother, conjured myself a paper and a pen, and got to writing.

My succinct letter to Barrett was written and off to

annoy him in two minutes flat. His response was terse, but I could feel his relief at hearing from me through the note he sent back.

Meet us at the door. We have much to discuss.

I really hoped he was referring to the portal door that brought us here, because after I latched onto my mother's hand and grabbed Niall's sleeve, that's where I took us. Yeah, there probably should have been a discussion about where we were going or who we were meeting, but I just didn't have the energy.

I left my mother to her cursing and Niall to his spluttering, walking straight toward the portal door. Yes, for a split second, I thought about walking through it and going to my house and taking a nap. I thought about just giving up on it all. But then Barrett walked through the door with Marcus behind him, and I just fucking lost it. I sprinted to them, letting the pair of them fall all over me in a group huddle. I then vaguely noticed Andras, Bernadette, and Atropos had followed them through.

Out of all of them, I expected my grandmother and father the least. I'd specifically requested Atropos' presence, and the fact that she actually came made me think hope wasn't actually lost. Maybe. Honestly, it was a crapshoot and we were all probably going to die. Who knew at this point?

After a few moments that seemed way too short, Barrett pulled back to look at me. "Darling girl, you look like you've been put through the wringer." He clucked his tongue as he tucked me under his arm, pulling me toward another door to the cottage. "How about some heavily laced tea and a chat?"

It wasn't like I was going to tell him no. I had reached the very end of my rope, and if Barrett was going to make me tea and give me a hug, I was all for it.

The cottage itself appeared ramshackle on the outside and a cozy little space on the inside. The furnishings were straight out of the 1950s but they seemed to be in good repair and clean. I wasn't going to turn my nose up at any of it. To the left of the room was a couch and several armchairs with cute little throw pillows dotting the corners. To the right was a bare-bones kitchen with an avocado-colored refrigerator, butcherblock counters, and a mammoth farm sink. In the window above the sink were several thatches of herbs tied together with twine which hung from a wooden shelf, their corresponding pots above each.

Someone appeared to live here. Took care of the place, too. Everything was clean and in good repair, and it had the distinct air of home. Not my home, but somewhere I could rest. Because we were in Faerie, I immediately assumed it was a trap, but Barrett was the one to suggest the place, so I let that go.

Before I could say "boo," Barrett had me curled up on the couch with a blanket tucked around my leathers, a cup of tea in my hands that was mostly booze, sandwiching me in between him and Marcus like they were holding me together by sheer force of will. That assessment probably wasn't too far from the truth.

I let Teresa do the explaining because I was tapped the fuck out. Over the last two weeks I had traversed Hell, lost my sister, gotten married, trekked through Faerie, found out I was a demigod, sealed up the Unseelie Court, and gotten my husband body snatched.

I was d-o-n-e—done.

"It seems that the warnings about demons in Faerie weren't bullshit," my mother began, and I snorted into my cup. She wasn't lying. "Alistair seems to be possessed by an entity known as Niall." She paused to let everyone process, and the Fae in question waved at the room like it was NBD.

I took that opportunity to snap my fingers and refilled my cup. It was straight booze this time, but could anyone really blame me? I was lucky I was self-healing, or my liver might have a few things to say. See? Silver linings were all around.

"Niall insists that he only possessed Alistair because he cannot communicate with us. Given his dire warning, I suggest we hear him out." At that, Teresa took a seat so Niall could have the floor. Andras, however, was not too keen on that.

"Do you know what she's gone through? Do you have even the faintest fucking clue?" Andras said, and I could only guess he was referring to me. I could've been wrong on that front, though. I wasn't the only one who watched Maria's mouth talk with another person's voice. I wasn't the only one to watch that get stolen from her along with everything else.

"I can't say I do. The only thing I know is if we don't retrieve Dušan before the Blood Moon rises, this plane and everyone sprung from it will cease to exist. If you're too busy worried about *feelings*, then I can't help you." Niall wasn't wrong, but it was likely the wrong thing to say to my father.

"My wife watched her daughter get possessed and we couldn't get her back. Max watched her sister die. And here you are, thinking we'll just hop-to with no assurances, no promise that the Alistair you stole will come back to her. Fuck you. Fuck you for thinking that my daughter can pursue another cause when she's been broken. Fuck you for thinking my wife can watch another one of her daughters' fight and die for a realm that has no love for them. Fuck you, buddy. Fuck you and the horse you rode in on."

If my hands weren't full of booze, I would have clapped. As it stood, I still had tears in my eyes, and I wanted to hug the shit out of him. Andras had never really felt like a dad, but dammit if he was vying for father of the year. Okay, maybe he wasn't the best dad on the planet, but he was trying.

Niall's eyes widened, affront written all over his face, but Andras didn't appear to give that first shit. "You are asking too much of her to watch you parade around in her husband's body. You ask too much of her... wait... who in the bloody hell is Dušan?"

I snorted in my cup again before speaking for the first time since I arrived. "He's my father. You know him as the god, Chaos. You know, the father of all the gods, where the Titans came from, Zeus' granddaddy. That guy. Supposedly he was dead, but according to Niall he isn't." I shrugged, taking another drink of my booze. It was yummy.

Everyone seemed surprised except for Atropos. She scowled at me. I was just drunk enough to give her a finger wave. "What's up, 'cuz? Wait, that's not right. Nyx is your mom, so that would make you my niece? This is one fucked-up family tree, am I right?"

Atropos sputtered before she broke out into a laugh. "You don't know the half of it."

"A daughter of Chaos. Really, it's not even a little surprising," Barrett volleyed, and I gave him a patented raised eyebrow. "Okay, so it's a little surprising, but just like the Fae business, it makes a whole hell of a lot of sense. You have way too much power for a simple Fae, Elemental or not."

"You're just mad you didn't know from the get-go," Marcus muttered, and squeezed me into his side.

"Fabulous. Her parentage is out in the open. How about we talk about the end of this realm and every single Fae that walks among the other eight." Niall was very interested in making sure we stayed on task—which considering the time frame, was a good call.

"She isn't going anywhere with you," Bernadette hissed, tossing a black lock off her shoulder as she stood. She was tiny compared to Niall, but the power held under her skin made her seem eight feet tall. "You say that she must retrieve Dušan, but he has other daughters. He has other sons. You want her to go, but you offer nothing in return. You want her to help you, but you offer no proof, nothing. We are to just trust you? After what you have taken and how you've injured her? I think not."

Ruh-roh. Gramma was pissed. It was about to get

heated in this little cabin. Which was sad because it was so nice and cozy.

"He speaks the truth." Atropos sighed. "The Fae Blood Moon only happens once every five hundred years. If Dušan is not here for it, there could be dire consequences."

"Way to be vague, Atropos," Marcus growled. "What kind of Fate are you? Yeah, let's just let a whole fucking realm tank and not say anything."

Then it was Atropos standing in anger, her red hair flying about her head in a halo of rage. I wondered if we should all start standing when we had a grand statement to make. "I do what I can. You know the laws I am bound to. You know, Marcus. So, don't sit there and tell me I'm doing a shitty job. I'm doing what I freaking can, okay? I'm here, aren't I?"

"Oh, for fuck's sake. Settle down. I'll just talk to him, okay? I've done it a couple of times already. I'll talk to the guy and see if we can get him out of whatever pocket dimension he made for himself, and we're good, right? Easy-peasy, lemon squeezy and shit." Yep, I was slurring the shit out of my words, but I had a feeling my message was clear enough. "Then you can give me back my husband, the world won't end, and things can calm the fuck down."

I took a little sip of what was left in my cup, and gently

set it down on the coffee table. Okay, so I had to close one eye and aim extra careful, but I at least attempted to set it down gently.

Then I snuggled into the blanket and closed my eyes, calling on the element that was as elusive and ephemeral as smoke. Spirit wasn't like the other elements. Those I could feel all the time here. They were like breathing or my heart beating—they seemed to flow into me without thought. Spirit only wanted to touch me when I was at my lowest, when I didn't have enough strength to go on.

Kinda like right now. I felt the pull at my chest, the heat of all the elements filling me, healing me... stealing my damn buzz, but whatever. Then it felt like I was falling for a second, a sensation I hadn't yet felt while contacting Dušan.

I opened my eyes, but he wasn't there. The forest that was blurry at the edges, the night sky that was too close and too far away at the same time, the wooden stump he sat on—those were all there.

But he wasn't.

Frantic, I called out, "Dušan! Come out. I need you!"

My eyes swept the tree line for the giant of a man with purple hair and lightning in his eyes.

But no one came.

Pulling out of the little pocket world took far too much

effort, and by the time I made it back to my body, I could tell something was wrong.

Teresa and Andras were holding onto me, forcing my arms to my sides as I thrashed. Also, I was on the floor— that was another clue that something was amiss.

"He isn't there," I croaked. "I called and called, but he isn't there anymore."

"We know, baby," Teresa murmured, pulling me to her as she wrapped me in her arms.

"What are we going to do?" I asked, but no one answered me.

CHAPTER THREE

"You can't do that anymore. You can't try to visit him again, Max." Bernadette's warning was clear, the command laced in every single syllable. "We almost lost you."

Lost me?

"What the hell are you talking about?"

Bernadette's—or rather Lilith's face—twisted, fear lining her expression. "If your parents hadn't have held you down, if I wasn't using all my power... Wherever Dušan was, it was pulling on you. I don't know the particulars—not really. Just... don't do that anymore. Maybe if he isn't there, the pocket world requires a new host?"

Well, that wasn't frightening at all.

"Not a host," Niall huffed. "Dušan is a creator of worlds. If he only managed to make a pocket world, then he has been recharging his power for centuries. It is possible that if he heard my call, then he has left that scant space he made for himself—it may be collapsing. You have to go back. If we know where that world is, we might be able to use it to find Dušan."

He wants me to go back to the place I almost got stuck in?

Eff that trash.

"Hell, no. Moreover, fuck you very much. I would very much like to not be stuck in some random pocket world with exactly zero exit strategy, thank you." I thought about what he said for about a millisecond before I added, "What do you mean "heard your call?" Does Dušan's pocket world have a landline, and I missed it?"

Niall leveled me with a glare so scathing, it was a wonder it fit on Alistair's face. "Do you honestly believe I have been waiting for four hundred years in the Unseelie realm without trying every single thing I could think of to bring him back? Do you think I have been twiddling my thumbs on vacation while I rot over there?" He brought up a good point, but he wasn't done. "I was Dušan's paladin. I was supposed to suss out things like this. I was supposed to protect him. If you think I'm going to let a piece of changeling trash bring down my charge, you are sorely mistaken."

Niall advanced on my parents as we knelt on the floor, a stance so threatening, it had the hairs on the back of my neck standing on end. I could feel the crackle of unspent magic in the air—the energy rising fast enough it felt like ants on my skin—but it wasn't me. No, that honor was reserved for Lilith. And make no mistake, this was *Lilith*.

Bernadette was a gorgeous grandmother. Lilith was the Queen of Hell. Ancient, ruthless, powerful.

And she was *pissed*.

"You would do well not to threaten her, Niall," she whispered. "Not by word or deed. Do we understand each other?"

Niall sneered—an expression quite at home on Alistair's face, but never with this much vigor. "I will do whatever I need to do to bring my King home. I will threaten, I will bargain, and I will kill. Do not mistake me, demon, I will complete my task or die in the trying."

And that was the point when I'd had just about enough. The tiny cottage was so pretty, it was too bad I was about to shake it into rubble. The ground danced a jig beneath us as I heard the crackle of lightning fizz and pop. And not outside, either. No, somehow, it raced over the walls before circling Niall's feet like a puppy.

"Do not mistake us, Niall. If you want us on your side, you're gonna have to be a bit less of a dick. We have the same goal. Getting ourselves killed in the process is no way to go about it. And offering me up as a test subject to a likely collapsing world is not going to win you any favors in this group. No matter whose face you're wearing."

I managed to pull myself up off the floor and walked out of the cozy little cabin.

Holding back tears, I took huge gulps of air as I tried to calm myself down. All that was Faerie smacked me in the face as I talked myself down from a rage. I was tired of feeling weak. I was tired of feeling like I had no control.

I was tired of the world throwing me under the bus time and time again.

It wasn't fair that so much had been taken from me—from us. It wasn't right that I couldn't—even for a full day—be happy with the progress we'd made.

I had a horrible thought right then. That I should just lay my sword down. That I should just plop down on my ass and let the world burn. Let Faerie and everyone in it burn to ash.

Maria was gone.

Alistair was overtaken.

I was tired. So tired.

"Don't do that," Lilith said from behind me, startling me so bad I jumped. I had been pretty far down on the shame spiral, so I wasn't too hard to sneak up on. Her black hair hung down her back as fire danced in her eyes.

"Don't do what?"

"Give up," she answered. "Don't you dare. You didn't

come this far—you didn't sacrifice this much to lay down and die now. I will get your husband back to you. We *will* win this fight. You *will* be happy again. I swear on everything in me, I *will* make this right for you. This doesn't get to happen to you. Not on my watch."

I wanted to believe her. I wanted to stand up and dust myself off and convince myself that I could press on.

I wasn't doing a very good job of it, if I was being honest.

"I want to believe you, but..." I couldn't even finish that sentence. How could I explain it so she would understand?

"But this was just one hit too many." Not a question, a statement of fact.

I nodded solemnly, turning away from her to stare at the enchanting forest filled with trees that could swallow me whole if I stepped wrong. The fog glistened against the leaves, little dots of light—which looked like fireflies but was probably a pixie of some kind—blinked in the darkened recesses of the foliage. It was beautiful and still. Creepy as all get out, sure, but beautiful.

This is what I'd be destroying if I sat down. This and every Fae I'd ever met. Every person of Fae blood that lived on Earth. This whole realm. It would all be gone.

I didn't know if I could be that callous, that oblivious to my own culpability and power to let everything burn while I watched. I didn't know if I could sit down and let it all go.

That's it. Get your shit together in that little brown paper sack you call a soul and fight, dammit.

Theeere she was. That was my conscience rallying for one more bout.

"That's better," Lilith said from behind me. "I was worried there for a minute."

I glanced over my shoulder at her, my expression probably more scathing than I intended, but whatever. "So glad you approve. Do you think we can come up with a different plan that doesn't involve me getting trapped in a collapsing pocket dimension to find Dušan?"

"Probably."

"Good."

It was then that I heard a smattering of running feet. Without a thought in my brain, I drew both athames, extending the blades to turn them into swords as I turned to the sound. Not a second later, Della, Aidan, Hideyo, and Striker bolted from the trees. Della had a dripping cut on her cheek and Striker looked like he'd been accosted, one of his sleeves was torn open and hanging from his shoulder.

Relief crossed each of their expressions when they saw me.

"What the fuck, Max?" Aidan barked after he caught

his breath, resting his hands on his knees as he sucked in air.

"What the fuck what? You're gonna have to be more specific."

Did I need to be that contrary?

No.

Did that stop me?

Also no.

"Why are you here? What is going on? Why does that forest of freaking teeth hate us? What. The. Fuck." All good points, I'd give him that.

"I needed to go to a meeting—that's why I'm here. The world is ending, is what is going on. And I have no idea why the forest hates you. Your guess is as good as mine." He opened his mouth to reply, but I held up a hand to stop him. "No, I don't want to go into it right now. Yes, you will get an explanation—just not from me. No, I'm not going to do something stupid—unless you think not stopping the world from ending is a good idea, then yes, I will totally be doing something stupid. And no, in case you were wondering, I am not okay. Did I cover everything?"

Aidan slowly closed his mouth, leveling me with an expression so concerned it was a wonder I didn't burst right into tears. Emotions were bullshit. "Yeah, Max. You covered everything. I'll talk to Lilith, yeah?"

"Yeah," I whispered, blinking furiously as I broke eye contact.

I let my gaze drift back to the forest. It was a wonder that just a few days ago I'd been more freaked about those trees than anything else. But it was Della who asked the question that brought me to my knees.

"Where is Alistair? We need him."

And then I was in the dirt, my knees and fingers digging into the earth as I just lost it. I could hear them asking what was wrong. I could feel their confusion and fear as the world churned beneath me and lightning cracked, and the wind whipped.

But I had nowhere to go.

No pocket place where my father calmed me down.

No husband to go to.

No Maria.

"Fine," Niall bellowed, yelling over the din. "If I give him back to you, will you cease this bloody temper tantrum?" It was said so scathing, I wanted to light him on fire. Granted, the world did settle down, so I couldn't exactly fault the guy...

Since he'd hijacked my husband, I so totally could.

Niall crouched in the dirt in front of me wearing Alistair's face like he had the right. It pissed me the fuck off.

"You take and take, and you still want more. You steal from me and have the nerve to say my grief is a temper tantrum? Give him back." I was shaking, my words barely passing my gritted teeth.

Niall sucked in a sharp breath through Alistair's nose. "I cannot communicate with you without a host. It is how I am bound." He swallowed thickly, remorse flitting over his face for a second before it was gone. "But if someone volunteers, I can use them instead. Had I known how important he was to you, I would have picked another host. I'm sorry, Massima."

I was full-on shivering then as hope bloomed in my chest. And then it was gone. Someone would have to take Alistair's place. I couldn't ask anyone for that.

"I'll do it," Andras offered, his booted feet stopping just in my line of sight. I stared up at him, watching as his golden eyes flashed.

"I can't ask that of you," I whispered, my face threatening to crumple.

"You didn't. I offered. I'm not going to let you down, Max. Not ever again."

I wanted to hug him, but I didn't get the chance. Niall opened his mouth and black smoke poured from it, exiting Alistair's body in a matter of seconds, his large frame falling in a heap on the dirt. It coalesced into creeping fingers, snaking into Andras' mouth and nose, filling him before I could blink.

An inky-black color filled the whites of his eyes for a

second before he blinked, shuddered, and fell to his knees. Andras shook his head once, twice, and then stood.

When Alistair had been possessed, he'd been out for a minute. Andras' body seemed to be taking it in stride. I met his gaze, a not-so-small tendril of fear snaking up my spine.

"I'm still me, you know," he said, probably trying to allay my fear but I wasn't so easily swayed. "I'm older and stronger than your Knight, kiddo. Niall is speaking to me and not through me. I know what we need to do."

A gust of a sigh passed my lips as I wilted in relief. I hadn't realized how tight I'd been wound until right then. Then my gaze fell to Alistair.

Now I was stuck waiting for someone I loved to wake the fuck up.

Again.

Aces.

CHAPTER FOUR

Time stretched like taffy as I watched Alistair's eyelids for movement. What was probably no longer than a few minutes felt like days. Years. Eons.

At the first flutter of movement, I held my breath, sending out a silent prayer to whatever deity that would hear me that he'd just wake up unharmed. And then I was staring into his baby blues, confusion clear in them for about a millisecond before they dialed themselves to pissed the fuck off.

Did I care about his rage? Hell. No. I cared that he was cognizant enough to be pissed. I pounced, my hands clutching his face as I looked him over. "Are you... you?"

His anger flowed away in an instant. "Yes, love. I'm me."

And since he was the smartest man alive, he brought his mouth to mine. I'd known after a single touch of his lips that he wasn't him. This kiss confirmed every hope I'd just prayed for. Inexplicably, I started crying. Even as happy as I was, the whole of the day had finally taken its toll on me. But all Alistair did was hold me to him, wrapping me in his arms and squeezing me tight.

When my tears ramped down, and after I'd likely scared the shit out of our entire party, I kissed him again. A sweet little kiss because I could. Because he wouldn't stop me.

Because it proved he was him.

I broke the kiss, met his gaze, and quipped, "The first year is always the hardest, right?"

Alistair snorted before squeezing the breath out of me as he crushed me to his chest. "I have to say, being married to you hasn't been dull at least." He pulled back to whisper in my ear, "I need to talk to you. Alone."

I gave him a slight nod and we stood. It was then that I realized everyone had gone back inside the cabin, leaving us to our reunion. I had half a mind to steal Alistair away so I could have him in a safe place without all the threats that loomed over us here. "We are alone."

"No, love, we are not. Eyes watch us here. What I have to say requires no audience."

That can't be good. "Okay. Do you remember everything?"

"I do. And I know quite a bit more. Let's talk to the group. If Andras is anything like me, he'll know quite a bit as well."

I nodded and he took my hand, leading me back to the cabin. My reluctance to go was gone now that he was with me. I wasn't okay—I might never be—but I could do this. I could press on.

The cabin was crowded with the addition of my paladins, every seat was full and even some choice floor real estate. They spoke in hushed whispers that I knew were about me. I had no illusions their choice of discussion topic, and I was fine with it.

Did they decide to lose it in the middle of a crisis? No. That was me.

I wanted to say sorry, but how does one apologize for flying off the deep end? "Sorry I'm a basket case" wasn't a greeting card I could just pick up at the grocery store.

"So, what did I miss?" I chirped, a fake sort of happy infused into my words. It rang false to me and everyone else in the room, but they had the good sense to ignore it.

"Niall suspects that Verena knows quite a bit about Dušan's whereabouts and what can be done to retrieve him," Andras began. "We will need to interrogate her. We have to know what she did to him before we can plan to retrieve him."

That meant I'd have to wake up Sleeping Beauty. This was not going to be fun.

THE DUNGEONS OF THE SEELIE COURT WERE unchanged since I'd walked out of them less than twelve hours ago. Funny. It had felt like years since I'd been down here. Since I'd freed the prisoners so wrongly detained.

Since I realized that Alistair wasn't Alistair. I squeezed his hand again, reassuring myself that he was really him and he was with me. Call me codependent if you want to, but I'd lost a shit-ton in not a large amount of time and I could not bear losing him.

Not after everything else.

Was I a nut-job right now? Absolutely. But hey, at least I was self-aware, right?

Verena lay sleeping on the stone floor of the cell Melody had once occupied. She was the only occupant of these cells, and other than Alistair and Aidan, I was alone to speak to her.

Verena didn't make sense to me. Not one bit. She had a family that abandoned her, but was accepted into a new family, in a new world. She'd gone from nothing to the ruling class in a place filled with magic, and still, that wasn't enough.

She wanted her booted foot on the throat of this world. And for what? Because her mommy didn't love her?

If that was a valid excuse, then I would have been razing cities and collapsing Hell by now.

I had to gather the courage to wake her and wondered if I could peek inside her mind without actually talking to her first. My honor wouldn't let me do that—stupid honor —and I contemplated the bars once more.

"What are you doing?" Alistair whispered in my ear, and even though I was troubled by the working I'd put on the cell, I smiled.

"Gathering courage, figuring out how to unravel my own magic, and questioning my life choices," I whispered back without taking my gaze from the Fae metal that housed Verena.

Alistair snorted, squeezed my hand, and said, "I have a feeling if you wanted in that cell you could just walk in there. No unraveling necessary. You are the daughter of Chaos, Max. Do you know who else is the daughter of Chaos? Nyx. Do you think those bars could keep her out?"

No. No, I did not.

Puffing out my cheeks to let out a huge breath, let go of Alistair's hand, and closed one eye, I winced and stepped forward. There was a fifty-fifty shot of this going horribly wrong. A rush of cold washed through me as I took another step, but then it was gone, and I was inside the cell.

One obstacle down.

I stared at Verena some more. With her Changeling magic gone, she had aged some. Not in a bad way, just in a way that spoke to how vain she was. There were faint lines fanning out from her eyes, a deep groove between her brows, and a pair of parentheses bracketing her mouth. Her scar was redder, too, like it was fresh instead of ancient. I vaguely wondered how she'd gotten it and why she chose to keep it.

I sat down on the stone bench, resting my elbows on my knees. Snapping my fingers, her eyes flashed open, the sleep spell I'd cast breaking, even though this room wasn't supposed to allow magic. Either I'd worked the spell wrong, or…

Or it was exactly as Alistair said. This cell would keep most out, but not someone like me.

Once Verena's gaze landed on me, she scrabbled backward—not because she feared me, but because she wanted time and space to make her next move. There was no fear on her face. None in her posture. She didn't care if I was able to take away her power with a snap of my fingers.

And why would she?

She killed the father of gods. Why would she believe anything else?

"I want to know what you did to Dušan." It didn't really matter if my statement was whispered or not, the power that leaked from my words made them a command.

A smile bloomed on her face as her eyes got that hazy quality of a fond memory. "You know what I did to your father, Massima. I killed him."

Dick.

"No, you didn't. I've spoken to Dušan. I know he managed to hold on. I want to know what you did to him specifically and in great detail."

She shrugged as if being in the cell with me was no skin off her nose, and I had the fleeting desire to turn her limbs inside out one by one until she told me. I'd done it to others. I couldn't say exactly why I did not relish doing that to her.

Was it because she was a girl? Was it because I had an inkling that torture wouldn't work? I couldn't tell, and I didn't like it.

"No, I don't think I'll tell you," she replied blithely. "I think I'll let you stew in your own ignorance."

This was a stalling tactic if I'd ever seen one. A stalling tactic that would earn her no favors from me. Rather than going the torture route—even though I really, really wanted to go the torture route—I snapped my fingers, yanking her to me. Fingers closing on her throat, my ass on the bench, her on her ass on the floor, I peered into her eyes. I'd peeked inside a Minotaur's mind without half the knowledge I had now. And he'd been a magical being.

Verena was no more magical than a human—not right then, anyway—and she knew it. The fear she'd eschewed before flooded her face.

"I've had a very bad day, preceded by a very bad few weeks, and a shit life. I'm pissed, tired, and hungry, and you are working my last fucking nerve. Answer the question, Verena. I'm not going to ask again." My whisper was as cold as ice, and if she had any sense in her brain, she would comprehend just how fucked she was.

Her face screwed into an expression that was three steps past mulish.

"So that was a no, then? Fine," I growled, clamping my hands to her head and drilling down into her brain. With no wards and no magic to stop me, I was bombarded by what she'd done.

The lives she'd taken.

The pain she'd caused.

And the pleasure and sick need she had to create more destruction. I didn't know what it was that caused this need, couldn't fathom the impetus that tipped her, but I didn't need to know that.

All I needed to know was what she'd done to Dušan.

She'd stolen power after power, changing into one creature after another, taking their power for her own. She started quietly at first until it started to snowball. Then she made her move. First by killing my brother and sisters, then by stabbing my father with the rowan branch before banishing him to the Unseelie Court.

But she didn't see him die. She'd only assumed he was dead because he hadn't come back. After that, she hunted my mother to the edges of Faerie, stabbing her too with the same branch that she believed killed a god.

She hadn't expected my mother to fight back. She hadn't prepared for the athame that ripped into her face. My mother had gotten away with me, but Verena had to recover, and since Zeta never returned, she assumed her dead as well.

She was right about my mother.

But I was becoming more and more certain, my father was alive.

I pulled back out of her head, only slightly aggrieved to find that Verena had not fared too well from my extraction. Blood dripped from her nose and eyes and ears, blood vessels had broken in her face, and with no magic to heal the likely ruptured organs and damaged tissue, she would die right here on the floor of this dungeon.

I was sort of fine with that. Then again, I wasn't fine. She hadn't suffered. She'd gotten off easy.

"Don't heal her, Max." Aidan's voice was a command from the other side of the bars. He knew me well enough to know that I would contemplate this course of action. I didn't know if I like that or not.

"And why not? She needs to pay."

"She deserves to be in Hell, love," Alistair answered for him. "I'll get word to the Knights. Make sure they know where to put her. I have a few friends who are very good at their jobs and enjoy their work. She will pay for what she's done. This I promise you."

I let his words appease me, and the bloodlust that I'd felt ramping up in my gut faded.

So we watched Verena take her last few labored breaths, the air squelching a bit as it passed once, twice, a third time between her lips before her body wilted and died.

And while I did this, I made a plan.

CHAPTER FIVE

After the day all of us had had, it was tough to slip my leash and enact my roughly formed plan. And while I appreciated everyone's need to check in on me to see how I was doing, their attention grated. I'd had to resort to saying I needed to go to the bathroom. Only Atropos leveled me with a look before taking her leave of the realm, insisting she needed to get back to her sisters.

This was likely the only reason no one figured out my bathroom gambit was a ruse.

Well, not exactly. I *did* need to go to the bathroom. It was just that after I'd taken care of business, washed my hands, and gave myself a stern pep talk, I did not go back to my friends and family. I snuck out of the castle and made my way back to that craggy crevasse where the rowan tree stood.

Well, I didn't sneak. I snapped my fingers and appeared where I wanted to be. I'd contemplated snapping my way to Dušan, but I had a feeling that it would not only *not* work, it would also maybe sorta kinda kill me.

The rowan tree appeared no different than when we'd left it those scant hours ago. Still tall, still whimsically mysterious. But the rowan tree wasn't exactly a tree at all. It was a sentient being named Aiyana the Eternal. And just as the name suggested, she was as cryptic and enigmatic and fucking ominous in a way that had the teeny tiny hairs on my arms standing on end.

And I would need to converse with this beautifully frightening being if I wanted my plan to work, because like an idiot, I'd made her create a gate to the Unseelie Court that no magic could break through. Not that I wanted to test that theory at all. My magic did not work near her, so I had a pretty good inkling that my abilities, as vast as they were, would do exactly bupkis to the scant door to the realm of monsters.

Rather than draw it out, I approached the trunk of Aiyana's tree, letting the power that made her suck me in. Instead of the blinding whiteness I'd experienced before, it was now a star-filled night. Galaxies peppered the sky with brilliant stars and swirling nebulas. I was so busy standing in awe of the beauty that it took a minute to realize Aiyana was standing beside me, her pale skin and blue horns glowing in the night.

"I see you appreciate the beauty of the night, Massima. I, too, enjoy the burn of the stars." It was as if she thought of the stars as her own personal crackling fireplace. I tipped up my lips at that oddity.

"I didn't expect you so soon after our last visit. Or maybe I did. With the Blood Moon so close, it would make sense why you would come to me. I take it you've come to make a bargain?"

That was the thing about conversing with a being that could read your mind. Subterfuge was futile. "I hadn't planned on coming this soon. I'd planned on eating, going to bed, and resting for a week. Then, only after I'd gathered the courage, would I come here. Today has not gone to plan in a bevy of ways."

Aiyana's smile was small but there. She thought I was cute, I'd bet. Like a Chihuahua or a Poodle.

I kinda wished she would have spilled the beans about the Blood Moon before we'd left the crevasse in the first place, but I wasn't going to scold her about it. I had a feeling there was a lot of shit she knew and hadn't shared.

"If you are willing to share, I would like to know about

the Blood Moon. What it is, why Dušan needs to be here, what the consequences are for skipping this year, etc."

"I see."

"In our deal, you spoke of teaching me about this realm, I figure since my tiny bit of knowledge says that this realm will cease to be in three days if I don't get my father back, this could be our first lesson." I paused before tacking on, "If you're amenable, that is."

Politeness was key here, but I may have been laying it on a little thick. Oh, well.

"What if I said I wish to skip over discussing the Blood Moon in favor of explaining how pixies were created, or whether worms were actually good for the fish to eat?"

I sucked in a breath, prayed for calm, and answered, "I would try to steer you back to the current matter at hand so I didn't die. Probably. Unless time dilates in here, then I'd pull up a seat and listen."

Maybe. But with my impatient ass, I'd probably fuck that up a little bit.

"You are one of the most self-aware deities I've ever encountered," she remarked, a ghost of a smile playing at the corners of her lips. "You do your best to be honest, not just with me, but yourself as well. You do not shy away from introspection, nor do you relish death and destruction. I wonder what you will be come in a millennium or three. Will you be jaded? Or will you stay as you are, doing better, trying to be better?"

I kind of hoped I would be the second option. I didn't ever want to be the jaded demigod with a thirst for blood. But did anyone really want to be the first option?

I doubted it.

But it didn't matter if I could technically live another year or a thousand more years if I couldn't get this Blood Moon bullshit sorted out. Me—right along with the rest of Faerie—wouldn't be breathing.

"Ah, yes, the Blood Moon. I suppose I shall tell you what you wish to know. Yes, the Blood Moon is real, it is a sacrifice to the universe. A payment Dušan must make every five hundred years to keep this realm whole."

"How does he pay it? What is the price? Who does he pay it to?" I thought those were good questions. Maybe I didn't have to break into the Unseelie Court and search for him. Maybe I could pay the price myself.

"The payment is never the same, and it cannot be a descendant of Chaos. It must be Chaos himself. He tried with one of your sisters, and even though she produced what was asked, the sacrifice was not accepted. Had Dušan not been there to right it, I fear we all might have been lost. As for who he pays it to, that I cannot say."

Not like she didn't know, but more like she couldn't

tell me. Something dawned on me—it really should have before now, but I was working on little sleep and a boatload of trauma, so I excused myself.

"You'll be lost, too, won't you? If I do not succeed."

Aiyana's smile stretched wide. "Perhaps. But perhaps not. I am here and not here. And I am not Fae, so I am not sure if I will go if Faerie collapses. I try to stay optimistic about these things."

I kinda wished she had the same level of motivation as the rest of us, but I could accept her honesty.

"So, to recap, the Blood Moon is real, it's dire if Dušan isn't here to pay the price, and I can't pitch-hit for him. Anything else I should know?"

"You have three days. If Dušan is not at the rowan tree by the time the moon hits its apex, the bargain will be void." All good things to know.

"Do you know where he is?"

She shook her head, her eyes sad. "I do not. Not exactly. I know he is beyond the wall. But the Unseelie Court is vast and treacherous. And dark. The light that shines here does not shine there. I cannot see."

"Well, at least there is a general direction. Will you let me pass? I won't insult you by trying magic on your roots. I know it won't work."

Aiyana contemplated this for a full minute. Well, I

could only guess she was contemplating it because she was silent, her eyes downcast.

"No. Not without a sacrifice of your own. I think I would like the life of a fawn—no, wait—a water dragon. Your friend Zillah will do. Yes. Bring me Zillah's head, and I will let you through."

I reared back, disgusted. "Absolutely not. I'm all for killing out of necessity, but you don't need a sacrifice. You want one. What the fuck is wrong with you?"

Aiyana smiled, lips pulled into a no-shit grin. "Do you know how many times I have asked that of deities and they just nodded without question? Do you know how many people in your shoes would not hesitate to kill a friend?"

I crossed my arms. "That better be pride in your voice, woman."

"I am no woman, and yes, it is pride. The fate of our world—your life—is at stake and you refuse to murder. Yes, I think I can make something of you yet, Massima."

"I hope that's your vague consent for passage. I've got a deity to find and not a lot of time to do it."

Aiyana nodded. "Three days. Don't let time slip away from you."

I wanted to say thank you, but I thought better of it. Fae or not, Aiyana was not a being I wanted to owe. "I appreciate your help."

Aiyana smiled wider and muttered, "Smart girl."

I didn't know if I felt all too smart, but I at least had a vector and a general plan. Go to Unseelie Court. Find Dušan. Haul ass back to the gate. Pray we make it in time for the Blood Moon.

As far as plans went, it was absolute shit, but it was what I had. I came back to myself at the foot of Aiyana's tree, the dirt sifting through my fingers as I wobbled to standing. Instantly, the hairs on the back of my neck prickled, and I knew I wasn't alone in this crevasse.

Shit.

Slowly, I glanced over my shoulder to see not just my husband but my parents, my grandmother, my paladins, Barrett and Marcus, and Striker all staring at me like I had just shit on their birthday cake. My mother, in particular, looked like she was ready to open-hand slap me.

Didn't they get that I was leaving them behind for a fucking reason?

Alistair approached cautiously because he was a smart man and he knew me. How long had we been together? A week? A month? How did he already know the right things to do?

How did he know that I was a stupid, fragile creature with too much power at my disposal and the emotional control of a toddler?

I picked the best person in the universe to marry, and it was by total accident.

"We won't be left behind, love. You are heading into enemy territory. You need more than just your power as backup."

"Three of you are demons. One of you is already possessed. What happens if I fail? What happens if I can't protect you? What happens if we don't all make it out? I can't handle one more person leaving me, but especially not you. You're asking me to take my whole world with me—put you all in danger right alongside me. I don't... I can't..." I shook my head. I was positive I'd rather die than do that.

"I have a working to circumvent the possession thing, darling," Lilith called. "We fudged it a smidge during Alistair's warding. I've fixed the error and tested with Niall. It works."

Teresa, who appeared calmer now that she'd gotten my explanation, stepped up beside my husband and said, "Everyone has protection charms and warding. We are armed, ready, and have a good idea where Dušan might be. With Niall's help, we might be able to find him sooner than we thought. But we need numbers, Max. Don't leave us behind out of a need to protect us. We are all signing up for this. It is our choice."

I wanted to rage at her that I couldn't keep her safe—

that I couldn't keep anyone safe, but that wasn't what she'd said. She knew the danger. She wanted me to allow them to accept it and fight, anyway.

"Okay," I whispered, conceding even though it burned my soul up to do it. "Let's go."

CHAPTER SIX

Aiyana saw much more than I'd given her credit for, because no sooner had the giant-assed group of us walk up to the tangle of roots that made the gateway to the Unseelie Court, did she part them so we could walk through. The hole was small, no bigger than a tractor tire, and all of us had to tuck ourselves into a ball to climb through.

Once on the other side—and only after the last of us crossed—did the roots seal shut again. The slight problem I found was I had no idea how to get back to the Seelie side once this was all over. The wall of roots that was visible from that side was gone, replaced by a stone cliff face complete with moss-covered boulders and ferns jutting out of the cracks.

Nope, not frightening at all.

The landscape was a dark forest, fog mingling at the bases of trees—and not the sparkly glitter fog either. No, this was a dark mist that seemed oily and caustic. The trees were gnarled and twisted like out of a fairytale nightmare, battered leaves and bracken littering the forest floor.

If I were being honest with myself, this was exactly what I'd figure the Unseelie Court would look like. Dark, ominous, threatening.

Super.

"We must go this way." Andras pointed to what I assumed was south if my internal compass was on point. Not that I trusted it completely in a place like this. I was tempted to leave breadcrumbs *Hansel & Gretel* style, but I was fresh out. Andras had a far-off expression on his face like he was listening to Niall speak inside his head. "Niall says that he has searched the Unseelie Court for four centuries, looking for Dušan. The pocket world he created for himself made it hard to pinpoint his location, but he can find him better now."

I didn't know how much faith I had in Niall, but if he had a lock on Dušan, we needed him. That was the only reason I followed after Andras as he listened to the Fae parasite inside his head. We, as a group, marched into the trees, and I was certain everyone—like me—was keeping an eye out for danger. Honestly, I was just waiting for one of those zombie-like creatures to pop out of the ground and fucking eat us.

But the farther we moved into the trees the denser they got. It was as if they were moving in closer to us, uprooting themselves to hem us in. I didn't like this. It felt like a trap. Like one of those military operations that funneled people into a centralized location before opening fire.

We were the fish and the trees were the barrel.

Unless I was being paranoid. That was an option, too.

I tugged on Alistair's hand as I whispered, "Is it just me, or are those trees getting closer to us?"

I was having a tough time not staring at the craggy bark, so when he squeezed my hand back, I peered over my shoulder at him.

"No, love. It's not just you. We are being herded."

I was super tempted to flex back, but I knew if I exploded this forest—which was probably filled with sentient trees—I would be taking lives and earning a whole host of attention we likely did not want.

Still, the trees moved so close it was getting harder to move forward. I was about to say fuck it and do something stupid when a thick tree no-shit pulled up its roots from the ground and stalked over to us. What was this, *The Lord of the Rings*? Hell, for all I knew it was a historical account.

The tree rumbled out a command, but because none of

us spoke tree, we had no idea what he was saying. Well, that was until Andras started translating. Likely it was Niall in his head translating, but that was just too confusing a concept to think about.

"He says that he is the Guardian of the Gate. Don't ask me what they call the gate because I cannot possibly pronounce it. Anyway, he says we do not belong here and may not pass. We are to go back where we came from and never darken this forest again. Essentially."

I wondered how much I should tell the tree about our business. It wouldn't do if everyone and their brother knew about what we were doing here. Then again, what kind of hope did we have if he didn't peacefully let us go?

"Does he have a name? Because calling him Treebeard would probably be considered rude."

"Not that he's said, but I think he can understand you. It's you who cannot understand him."

Fabulous.

"I'm Max," I called to the giant tree. Seriously, he was a moss-covered, gnarled mammoth tree with twisted bare branches and at least a hundred feet tall. "I am a daughter of Chaos and we need to find him. This is the only reason we are here. If you let us pass without incident, we will be peaceful. If not, I cannot say what will happen. If we do not get Chaos back, this world will end. All of Faerie will die. I want to be peaceful, but I'll cause a ruckus if I have to."

The tree spoke in his grunted language, the garbled consonants low and vicious.

Andras didn't translate immediately, so I stared at the side of his face until he started talking. I could tell he did not want to tell me whatever the tree said. I was also pretty sure I did not want to know whatever it was that Andras didn't want to tell me.

I had a feeling, though, that whatever Treebeard said was sort of imperative to the current situation, and if Andras didn't spill the beans, I was going to get pissed.

"While he understands your plight—and our mission— no Seelie Queen has stepped foot in the realm for four hundred years. Verena imprisoned them here, and..." Andras trailed off. I was pretty sure I was going to start yelling if he didn't get the fucking lead out and cough up the rest.

"What's the rest, Andras? Kinda on a time crunch here," I snapped, but I didn't let my magic loose, so at least there was that.

Andras mumbled the rest, his words coming out in a rush, but I still got the gist. And I better not have heard what I thought I did. "Say again?"

"He requires a person to stay behind as collateral so you will do as you say."

I was about to start yelling at a sentient tree that he could take his request, fold it up into little corners, and shove it up whatever gnarled bark hole he called an ass when Striker spoke up from behind me. "I'll stay."

Mouth hanging open, I whipped my head to stare at him. He was already shifting through our little crowd. He stopped when he reached me, pausing to speak low into my ear. "You need someone to make sure the way back is clear, Max. It wouldn't hurt to have a fire-breathing dragon as your clutch player if this decided to go sideways," he offered, and if our history was any indication, things always had a way of going sideways on us. Then he continued, and his next bit broke my heart a little—not because it wasn't true, but because it was. "Plus, it's not like anyone trusts me. For good reason, I know, but still. I have to earn that back. I can do this."

I really hated it when he spoke logic and I was being the emotional one. Really. It was so rude of him. Heaving a sigh, I let him pass, leveling the tree with my very best of glares.

"He had better be in the exact condition I left him in when I get back. No spells for sleeping, no immobilization, no nada. Do not torture, maim, injure, or kill him. There better not be so much as a splinter in his finger, or you will answer to me. Do you understand?"

The tree, with his craggy face appeared kinda surprised

a woman less than a tenth his size was threatening him. Still, he nodded, muttering some grunts and warbles to Andras.

"He agrees about everything but the splinters," Andras interpreted, and I couldn't help it, but I snorted.

"Fine, if he gets a splinter in his finger—as long as it's not poisoned and will kill him or make him sick or whatever—then I won't raze this entire forest. Happy?"

A few more grunts which Andras translated, "Yes, he agrees."

Fabulous.

One tree negotiation down, one member of the team sidelined, and one monster of a trek to go.

Once the tree guardian—or whatever the hell he was—let us pass, it was easier going. The trees backed off from us, and soon we were out of the forest altogether and following a rocky outcropping that had to be a cliff. A wide gorge sat to the east, the craggy rocks sharp and foreboding. It was way too wide to cross in some places—even with magical assistance—so we continued south for a bit. I was tempted to just travel, but I had a feeling expending magic here was a good way to pop up on someone's radar, and the walk had been smooth so far.

I didn't want to spoil it before we'd found our bearings.

That was until we came upon a slender vine bridge at one of the thinner spots in the gorge. It seemed rickety, sure, but if it would hold, then we could get this show on the road, and maybe get Dušan back before the world imploded.

That was before I noticed the figure standing in the middle of it, blocking our way.

"I swear to the Fates, if that's a troll, I'm out of here," Aidan griped, and I had a tough time holding in my snicker.

"Nah, too skinny to be a troll," Hideyo remarked. "Probably a river Fae."

I hadn't noticed it before now—because I wasn't stupid enough to get close to the edge—but the gorge housed a pretty substantial river. Holding onto the vine railing for balance, I peered over the side. Swirling azure water raced swiftly through the crack in the earth, the white froth of rapids pummeling the sides of the nearly kissing mountains.

The water roared at us, and I wondered why I hadn't noticed before now. Still, I did not want to bargain with a river Fae, and I did not want to potentially lose another member of my team to whatever bullshit sacrifice or riddle or whatever such bullshit was in store for us.

Still, I was the de facto leader, so I yanked up my big girl panties and tried not to vomit as I made my way to the Fae barring our way.

I was shaky, sweating, and close to freaking the fuck out by the time I made it to the middle of the bridge. Okay, so sue me. I did not like rickety bullshit vine bridges that could snap at any second and leave me plummeting to my eventual drowning.

The river Fae—or that's what I was assuming they were—was silent. It was tough to put a finger on their gender, so I mentally settled on they. With green skin and bulging black eyes, they should have been ugly but weren't, and while their features were dialed to fish, it was in conjunction with pouty lips and cheekbones sharp enough to cut glass. With their iridescent scaled neck and flowing purple hair, they were weirdly beautiful.

Still. I did not want to be on this bridge, and I did not have time to dawdle.

"What do you want?" I asked impatiently, while the fish-person blinked at me, bored.

Bored. Like being on this stupid vine bridge hanging over certain death was a super-fun way to spend a lazy Sunday. Fucker.

The fish person regarded me a few moments longer before I got really pissed off.

Don't use magic. Don't use magic. Don't use magic.

A sly smile crossed their fish lips before they spoke. "I want what all dark Fae want. Death and blood. Give me the life of who you hold most dear, and I will consider letting you pass."

"Yeah, those terms don't really work for me, so I'm gonna have to decline. Have fun on your bridge, though," I said snidely, snapping my fingers and transporting myself to the other side of the gorge.

And then I got cocky—which thinking back on it was probably why what happened, happened. I gave the fish person a shitty little finger wave and blew them a kiss, flaunting the fact that I did not need their fucking bridge.

About three seconds after I did that, the ground eroded away from beneath my feet, and I was falling into the churning waters below.

CHAPTER SEVEN

The fall seemed to take for-fucking-ever. The river hadn't appeared to be that far down, but in the fall itself, getting to the water seemed to take a bloody age. I actually had the time to kick myself for being an asshole, forgive myself because they asked for blood and death, and then fret about what the fuck I would do when I actually got to the water.

Maybe I was processing shit at lightning speed. Maybe time dilated. Whatever. The closer I got to the surface, the more I could see the creatures thrashing beneath the water's depths.

I had a whole host of not-okay thoughts about that. I wanted to call on the water element, wanted it to help me, but as my feet broke the surface of the shockingly cold water, I couldn't think of anything else besides the needlelike sensation of near-freezing water slamming my senses like a wrecking ball.

In a moment of panic, I kicked, trying to get to the surface, but no matter how hard I kicked, I couldn't reach the air. Not quick enough to save my lungs from burning like molten lava in my chest, I realized that I'd gotten turned around in the fall. I tried turning myself around, but shadows surrounded me, the churning rapids kicking me about as I struggled to just go up.

I couldn't find the surface, I couldn't...

A flash of blue scales had me trying to back up. Well, that was until I saw a familiar face. Some might fear a giant blue sea serpent reaching out to grab you, but Zillah was a friend—a friend who had saved my ass in Hell, no less. His giant, yet gentle talon wrapped around me and we went up.

I coughed and sputtered as I broke the surface, vomiting up water when Zillah gave me a gentle squeeze. Only when I could breathe again, did I assess our surroundings. We were on a craggy shore. Or, I should say I was on the craggy shore while Zillah filled up the whole of the cove, his long dragon body curling in on itself like a pile of snakes. The river rushed past us, the gorge so far in the distance it wasn't even funny.

"River Fae are dicks, am I right?" I croaked, pushing myself up from the rocks, my leathers and weapons squelching as I did so. I was of the opinion my "no magic" edict was complete bullshit. Zillah gave me a low snuffled sound that I took as agreement. "Want to give me a ride? I need to make sure that bridge prick isn't trying to bargain with my friends."

Zillah gave me another snuffled grunt and bowed his head. When I hesitated, he reached out with a clawed foot and plopped me on his crown. I used his spiraled horns as handlebars—even though they were the size of freaking tree trunks, so I really only held onto one—and we were off.

Zillah had absolutely no trouble snaking up the thrashing river, the rapids churned against him. His huge body took the force in stride. Luckily, he kept his head above the surface—otherwise he probably would have lost me he was going so fast. The spray of the water hit me in the face, but I didn't care. This felt like flying, like soaring, and in a way, I was.

When the bridge came into sight, I realized a couple of things. One, my group of friends could not be left unsupervised, like ever. And two? I was really fucking happy they were on my side.

Aidan and Alistair were sawing at the fast-growing vines on the east side of the gorge, trying to unseat the water Fae. Andras, Della, and Bernadette had already traveled to the other side and were sawing from their end.

Teresa and Barrett were concocting some sort of spell on the cliffs from twigs and fucking berries, and Hideyo and Marcus were in their other forms ready to throw down.

All through this, the river Fae seemed unmoved, and while I figured they saw something like this quite often, I had to admit, I was more than a little touched that my friends were ready to burn a motherfucker down if need be.

The Fae yawned—no shit, *yawned*—at them until they caught sight of me rolling up on a fucking water dragon. Now, I knew the gorge was deep, but I had no idea how big Zillah was until he rose up as high as he could go, and the both of us were looking down on the river Fae.

"That. Was. Rude," I said finally after waiting for the apology I was owed. Seriously. That water was fucking cold.

Giant fish eyes wide, the Fae knelt on the vines—do not ask me how, that lone action defied everything I knew about physics as a whole—and stuttered out a hesitant, "Ma-majesty?"

I really hated that title, but if it got this prick to move, I was all for it. Then I had a thought. "How do you know who I am?"

Fish-person frowned in confusion. "The water serpent, Majesty. Zillah only serves the children of Chaos. He is bound to protect them."

Huh. Well, you learn something new every day. "Are you going to let my friends pass and quit being a monstrous dick? Seriously. *The life of who you hold most dear? Was that even necessary?*"

Trembling, they answered, "I was charged with keeping people out of the Court. Very few wish to sacrifice their loved ones, Majesty. I was just doing my job."

I thought about that for a second and realized I couldn't fault them for it—especially since I'd been a bit of a dick about it.

"Those rules do not apply to me and my team, let them pass, but keep your post. We'll be coming back through soon enough. If we have a tail, you can drown as many of them as you want. Cool?"

Fish-person nodded and snapped their fingers, transforming the rickety vine bridge into an arched stone one that was about as wide as a single-lane track. I pulled a Striker move, letting out a whistle for my friends to get the lead out.

Things were tense as my team from the east crossed over to the west side of the gorge, passing Fish as they went, but Fish never moved, only kept their head low.

When Alistair and Aidan passed, though, I got an expression of relief from my husband and a censuring "What the fuck?" from Aidan.

That was fair. I probably should not have antagonized an unknown Fae in the Unseelie Court. That was my bad.

"Do you have a name?" I asked the Fish-person and they hesitated. I amended my statement. "Rather, what can I call you?"

"Pip, your majesty. I appreciate your leniency." They paused, their big eyes filling with relieved tears. "The Seelie Queen was a monster in a pretty dress."

I almost wanted to cry at that admission. Jesus, fuck, Verena had deserved to die.

"She's dead, you know. She isn't coming back."

Just like the people in the castle had, Pip wilted in relief. This bit of Faerie had been locked away for centuries, and even this one river Fae was relieved she was dead. What the fuck had she done to these people?

"I will keep my post, Majesty. I will do as you say. I give you my word. Thank you for not..." Pip trailed off, unable to finish the sentence.

"For not being a raging bitch on wheels? Yeah, glad I could be of service. Stay safe, Pip."

With that, Zillah and I moved to the other side of the gorge, and I disembarked his head. He rested his chin on the ground, his eyes pleading as he moved no closer. That made me have a thought. Striker could change between his human and dragon form. I had yet to see Zillah in anything other than this. Even when it seemed he had something to tell me.

Even when he had time to change.

And he had no issue going from one realm to the other. Hell, Faerie. He could have probably shown up on the Earth realm if he wanted to.

"Are you stuck like that?" I asked, unable to just walk away from the serpent who saved my life. I couldn't say why exactly. It was like I needed to make sure he was okay.

Zillah let out an answering chuff, giving me a slight nod.

"Do you have a human form?" I whispered, hurt in a way I couldn't explain at this big beast being caged in his own skin.

Zillah nodded with more vigor, his motion dislodging rocks and earth from the side of the cliff.

"Do you need help changing back?"

Zillah's face was a picture of pleading: his giant scaly face, and huge blue eyes. Shit. I totally had to help.

I thought about it for probably less time than I should —the spell was probably older than I was. But I had to help. Zillah had saved my life twice—well, probably a third time if that Kelpie was planning on killing me.

"Max, what are you doing?" Lilith called from a few feet away. She sounded wary and censuring.

"Trying to figure out how to turn Zillah back to human again," I answered simply—like what I was doing was a totally normal thing to be doing in the middle of the Unseelie Court with people probably clocking our every move.

Still.

Faintly, I caught sight of the tracery magics weaved into his flesh. I was right. The spell was older than I was. Hell, it was older than Andras, probably. And done by a demon?

"It is not smart to meddle in these things, Max. He is likely that way for a reason." Andras' tone was more wary than his mother's had been.

Bullshit. I smelled bullshit. A heaping pile of it.

"This dragon has saved my life twice now. I know he's a friend. Would you stand idly by when one of your friends was hurting?" At his abashed expression, I pressed on. "I thought not."

I turned back to Zillah, studying the magic once more so I could unravel it. Yeah, I probably had god-power and could undo it with a snap of my fingers, but this spell was delicate and intricate, buried in his flesh for centuries, eons maybe.

"Maxima, do not mess with that dragon."

Funny. When she told me not to, that was exactly what I wanted to do. Far more than ever before. I looked her in the eyes, leveling her with a glare as I wondered why she didn't want me to free a sentient creature of a prison.

Then I raised my hands, snapping my fingers in open defiance of her warning.

At that, her face went white like I'd drained all the blood from her body and then some.

It was entirely possible I had just fucked up.

Again.

Go me.

CHAPTER EIGHT

Okay, so pissing off my grandmother seemed to be a pastime of mine. And maybe I'd never gotten those dick toddler moves out of my system when I was a kid. But I couldn't pay too much attention to the fit she was about to throw. No, I was watching an impossibly large water dragon that had been stuck in his animal form for who knew how long, condense his body into a human-sized pocket of a person.

Zillah's transformation was hurting him if his blood-curdling-roars-turned-screams were anything to go by. His body bent, contracted in on itself, slithering further onto land before the trunk of his body shrunk to the appropriate size. He writhed on the ground as his body changed shape, and when it was done, he appeared no bigger than I was and no older than a teenager.

I knew for certain Zillah was older than I was by likely eons.

Gasping for breath, he stared up at the sky with his odd blue eyes. Still with their slit pupil and strange too-bright-blue hue, he blinked there for a few minutes, unmoving. A shock of dark hair topped his head, and coupled with his pale skin, his eyes seemed to glow. He was dressed in fighting leathers that looked ancient, and how they'd held up this long was anyone's guess.

"I can't believe you did that, Maxima. I can't believe you just…" Lilith trailed off, shaking her head. "You just stared me right in the eyes and snapped your fingers. What the fuck?"

I sighed, the disappointment clear in my tone as I replied, "Do you know that with how many times you have lied to me in the last year, I can tell when you're doing it now? That I know when you're hiding shit and being an untruthful snot? I don't like that I know what your tell is, Lilith. So if Zillah is some crazed beast, now is the time to state your case."

Lilith huffed before crossing her arms. Defensive much? "He is not a crazed beast. He just should not have been turned back. His job is not done, and that is not the bargain we agreed upon you slithering little snot," she said, turning from me to address Zillah directly. "You knew you agreed to watch over him until the war, Zillah. I can't believe you conned your way out of it with a pair of doe eyes and a whine. Honestly. Is nothing sacred?"

Zillah took that moment to quit blinking at the sky and speared Lilith with a glare so cold it was a wonder she didn't freeze on the spot. He didn't appear much older than sixteen. He cleared his throat—after years of disuse, it made sense—and growled a single word in a thick accent I couldn't place. "Conned?"

"Yes," Lilith insisted. "Conned."

Zillah took a few seconds to get his bearings and stood for the first time on two feet in who knew how long. He was unsteady as he came back to himself, but he quickly rose to his full height. He was my height, but then again, Zillah didn't seem full-grown, either. "You are the cheat. You neglected to mention that the war would never come as long as Lucifer stayed in his cell. That I would be stuck in my dragon form until the end of days, patrolling the rivers until the worlds ended. You tricked me, and you know it, Lilith. I will not watch over your father's cell another minute. I don't care if he is a child of Chaos."

That was a lot of info to digest. To combat the utter shock, I conjured myself a chair—the same green velvet one I'd conjured myself plenty of times when I was stuck some place I did not want to be—and a tub of popcorn. This firework show wasn't over, and I was going to listen to every fucking word as it played out.

My husband, however, was not as inclined to watch the show.

"Lucifer's daughter? Child of Chaos? What in the bloody hell is he talking about, Lilith?" Alistair growled.

"That's what I'd like to know as well," my mother hissed. "Tell us, Lilith, what is this poor soul talking about?"

There was a lot of rage directed at my grandmother. Well, except for my paladins who were digging their hands in the tub of popcorn as all of us stuffed our faces with buttery goodness. This was better than reality TV. Andras seemed torn, like he wanted to defend his mother, but there wasn't anything to say.

This was a big fucking secret.

"My father is Lucifer, yes. My mother is Nyx. Yes, I'm the bastard child of two gods. Yes, Lucifer is remanded to the pit, which is located underneath the river Styx, which Zillah patrolled daily as was his bargain."

Well, that was a story not in any religious text I'd ever heard of. Wait a minute.

"Isn't Nyx a daughter of Chaos? And Lucifer is a son of Chaos, and they did the nasty? *Ewwww*."

Lilith rolled her eyes. "They were not conceived and born. They were made into existence with a snap of Dušan's fingers. It isn't like you. You were born, and had they been the same as you, then you'd be right. *That* would have been gross."

Okay, I could see that. Plus, it wasn't like there weren't more instances of straight-up weirdness as far as gods were concerned.

"So, you're like... my niece? That's super weird. I don't like it. I'm gonna ignore that piece of our relationship, cool?"

"Please do. The last thing I need is you lumping me in with Atropos in the family territory."

I snorted. "You're sisters with Atropos. How does that feel?"

Lilith sighed and searched the heavens for what looked like patience. "It feels like Lucifer is my father, and since he raped Nyx, and that's one of hundreds of reasons why he's in that bloody cell, I have to say, I could do without it." Lilith shifted her gaze from me to Zillah, whispering words that hurt my heart. "I did a lot of not-so-nice things to get him locked away, Zillah. I know you remember what it was like under his rule. I know you remember those days, even though they are far behind us. I don't want to go back there. Ever."

Something dawned on me as the popcorn in my mouth turned to sawdust. "The angels helped, didn't they? That's why the Armistice is in place—why you refused to break it. Even for me."

"It was a dark time for all the realms. Dušan could not bear to kill his son, but he was out of control, so we made a bargain with the angels that there would be no more bloodshed in exchange for..." Lilith paused, seeming to steel herself against what she was about to say. "In exchange for one thousand angel souls, we promised that Lucifer would be locked away. Guarded forever by a being that could not die. And no more angels would ever die at our hands."

Wow. Just... wow.

"I reinfused the magic over time, making it stronger as the years pass. I do this so my mother doesn't have to—not that I know where she is these days. Nyx has a bad habit of not staying in touch."

The demons and angels sacrificed a thousand souls to keep Lucifer in his cage. Holy. Fucking. Shit.

"I think my brain just exploded," Aidan muttered, and I agreed wholeheartedly.

"Way to bury the lead, Lilith. I take it these sacrifices were done the hard way?" The pain in her eyes when she finally met my gaze felt like a brand. Yeah, the sacrifices were done the bloody way and she didn't like it one bit. Even eons later, she still regretted them.

I wanted to be charitable about it, but *fuuuuck*. I also wanted Zillah not to be imprisoned, but holy fucking shit, he needed to get back to his post.

That thought was dashed almost as it filtered through my brain.

"I can't go back," Zillah whispered, wilting almost on the spot. "I'm supposed to stay with Massima. I'm supposed to be here."

Alistair plopped his ass on my ottoman and pinched the bridge of his nose. *Yeah, my brain hurt, too.*

"Why must you stay with her, Zillah?" my mother asked, her eyes scanning our surroundings for threats instead of looking him in the eye.

Zillah ran a hand through his short hair before patting it down in a gesture that was probably a nervous tick before he no longer had hands. "I don't know why I must. I know you put me in that river because my mind is safe from Lucifer. I know any other dragon would have succumbed to his whispers ages ago. I know that is the only reason why I got the job. *I know.* But something told me to stay with Massima. Something calls to me when she is in trouble more than any other child of Chaos. I am supposed to be here. And that is where I'm going to stay. Bargain or no bargain. Cage or no cage."

With that, I stood, snapping my fingers again to get rid of the chair and popcorn. There was no way I could eat another bite after what he'd revealed.

"Welcome to the team, Zillah." I offered him my hand. Instead of taking it, he took a knee instead. "No, no. No bowing. It's weird. And call me Max."

We left the cliff, moving west toward whatever the hell directions Andras was getting from Niall. I hadn't heard too much on Niall's opinion about Zillah and the current predicament we were in. Lucifer's cage—while reinforced with magic—had been left unguarded. Given what we knew about Soren and his draining of the boundaries to Hell, I wasn't super confident we didn't need to investigate that shit pronto. Too bad we were stuck following a Fae parasite into enemy territory.

The barren cliff gave way to more gnarled forest which then gave way to a craggy valley filled with razor-sharp rocks and slippery slate. Honestly? If I didn't know better, I would have confused the joint with Wales. It reminded me of this little town with too many damn consonants in the name that I couldn't pronounce if I wanted to. It was all sharp mountain inclines and slippery wet slate. One wrong step and you could fall off the fucking mountain. This was exactly like that.

That little town was beautiful but deadly. Just like this.

We'd been walking for a little while, the silence only broken by displaced rocks or the odd snuffling from Zillah that seemed so out of place when he wasn't a giant water dragon.

Alistair hooked his hand at my elbow and drew me back. Worry was stamped all over his features, the pair of lines between his eyebrows carved deep.

"I still need to talk to you. And, love, I think it might be urgent. Can you"—He mimed snapping my fingers —"and make them not be able to hear us?"

I nodded and snapped away—not taking their hearing away completely, like I'd once done to him, but making them not hear us as a whole.

"That should do it. Go on." To say that I was nervous was an understatement.

And I was proved right not a second later when Alistair confirmed the pit of dread I'd been feeling since I turned Zillah back to human.

"I don't think Lucifer is in his cage anymore."

CHAPTER NINE

I wanted to have a stiff upper lip about the current situation, but I was skating the razor's edge of sanity. First Micah, then Samael, Elias, Soren, and Verena... Was this the natural progression? Why not just get to the big boss and call it good?

Lucifer was probably out of his cage. *Yeah. Because that's exactly what we needed. Were locusts and murder hornets coming too?*

I was really glad no one else but Alistair could hear my crazed, semi-hysterical laugh. Still, the expression on Alistair's face when my cackle reached its crescendo probably threw in the final nail in my sanity's coffin.

I had officially cracked.

After wiping up my tears of mirth, I focused on his face, willing a teensy bit of sanity into myself. If this was actually a thing, trying to fix it should probably be penciled in at the top of my to-do list.

"Why do you think he's out?" I managed to ask, trying not to bust out in a fit of giggles as I pondered the idea of ding-dong-ditching a Fate's doorstep. Seriously. They'd shit all over my life, it was their turn.

Alistair shook his head as he frowned at me, his brow screwed up like he was searching his mind. "Niall was in my head. When you possess someone—or someone possesses you—sometimes you can access their mind before they throw up their wards." Alistair winced because whatever he was trying to access in his memories wasn't an easy thing to get to. "Before he shut me out—I caught a glimpse of something. I didn't know what it was at the time. It was a metal box, broken open. The box was old, under water, with the door thrown wide. I didn't put it together until after Lilith said where Lucifer was. I think Niall has known where Lucifer is for some time. I think this might be a ruse to… To I don't know what. But I don't trust him, and I don't think you should, either."

In a way, it made sense. Too many bad guys led to another bad guy. Too many were interconnected in a web of conspiracy and lies. Too many threads tied to the other.

"I think Lucifer slipped his leash when Dušan became stuck in his pocket spirit world, and I think he's been biding his time or... maybe gathering power. I think he's here, and I think Niall might be leading us into a trap."

"But the Blood Moon. Aiyana said it was true. Did he just use it to his advantage?" I asked because it was important to note that we still needed to get Dušan back —probably more now than before if Lucifer was on the loose.

Barrett took that moment to break into our little huddle. I knew he would probably be the first person to notice when he couldn't hear a particularly juicy conversation and come investigate. The snoop.

"I know you did something to my ears, Maxima. Fix it," he ordered, and I rolled my eyes as I snapped my fingers.

"You're too nosy for your own good," I griped once he could hear me. I pressed a kiss to his cheek as I skirted around him. "Alistair is going to fill you in. I have a pot to stir."

I threaded my way through our group, not walking too quick or too slow, not tipping my hand as I got closer to Andras. There was no way I was going anywhere without some cold, hard answers, and I'd pry them out of the Fae's mind myself if I had to.

That said, Teresa was going to be a problem. Rather than go into everything, I whispered, *"Somnum,"* rendering her unconscious before I enacted the next part to my hastily constructed plan.

Andras whirled, his gold eyes flashing before he started to dissolve into smoke. *Not today, buddy.*

Before he could completely devolve into his other form, I pounced, clapping my hands together, sending my power out to stop his change. The shockwave of the spell brought him to his knees, and before he could move against me, barbed vines sprung from the earth, wrapping around his limbs all the way up his body.

Now, all I had to do was get Niall out of my father's brain.

Should be a piece of cake.

I glanced over my shoulder to find that not only had I knocked my father on his ass with that little clap, I also brought just about everyone else to their knees as well. The only person left standing was Lilith, and she was none too happy about my current renegade antics.

"What in the bloody hell was that, Maxima?" Her voice was so loud nearby birds took flight and a bit of the ground around her feet shook. I guessed I wasn't the only person to inherit that bit of magic from Dušan.

"Andras has a parasite in his head, on that we agree, yes?" I asked her calmly, using the same tone I'd affect if I were calming down a feral dog.

"*Yes,*" she hissed back, no calm in the least.

"Now, I assume since Niall is Dušan's supposed paladin, he would know about Lucifer and his cage. Yes?"

Lilith pressed her lips together so hard they were white around the edges but gave me a short, terse nod.

"Well, Alistair informed me he saw an open cage in Niall's mind when he was possessed. An open cage at the bottom of a body of water. Meaning Lucifer is out. Meaning Niall knows this. Meaning this whole fucking thing is likely a trap or a ruse or some other such bullshit." I took a deep breath before my voice turned cold. "Meaning I'm getting his parasitic ass out of my father's brain, and I'm not going to be nice about it. Any questions?"

Lilith's eyes flashed coal black for a single second. From pupil to sclera, everything was black as the very pit of Hell before she took a single, measured breath to quell her shaking. Lilith feared her father. I had never seen her scared. Not once.

That was not comforting in the least.

"Knowledge is power, right? We can't know what he knows if he's inside Andras." She nodded, a single, sharp bow of her head, and I got to work.

With Alistair, I was hesitant to do this—forcibly evicting Niall—but with Andras I had no such compunction. Now that I knew his lineage, my worry about his survivability was practically nil. So I flexed my power as I slapped a hand to Andras' head, drilling down deep into his mind where I knew Niall resided.

Don't get me wrong, I tried not to see the bevy of images flooding my brain. The death, the sacrifices, the— *gag*—relationship with my mother.

Only when I felt the Fae writhing in his mind, did I start my spell. *"Exiens e tenebris in lucem prodeunt."* *Come forth out of the darkness and into the light.*

I repeated these words over and over, forcing my will into Andras' brain until it reached Niall, until I felt my spell wrap around him. Until I snared him in my thrall and yanked, pulling him free of Andras' brain.

Niall began to materialize. Black smoke fell from Andras' lips and nose just like it had when Alistair was freed. Only then did I pull out of Andras' mind, only then did I snap my fingers, binding Niall to his corporeal form with a single thought.

I was glad I did because he tried to dematerialize, likely trying to inhabit someone else.

Not on my watch, buddy.

With a wretched scream, I leapt at Niall and tackled him to the ground. But Niall had been fighting a lot longer than I had, and he rolled with me. I was up and over his body and flying through the air in less than a second. I may have tasted dirt there for a little bit, but I found my feet, ready to face him.

Only I wasn't the only one on my feet. No, Lilith and Andras flanked his left side, Aidan and Hideyo his right. Alistair and Barrett were bearing down on his front while a phased Marcus, a still half-asleep Teresa, and still-human Zillah were covering his back. Weapons drawn, teeth bared, talons at the ready, no one was letting Niall get anywhere.

Not today.

I loved my little family.

I approached the group, squeezing in between Alistair and Barrett to face Niall. His odd smoky face was scared. Hell, I would be too if I were facing down this lot.

"You don't get to do this to us. You don't get to lead us into peril. You don't get to hold everything back while we risk our lives," I whispered, knowing he could hear every single word I was saying. "You do not get to lie by omission. Not about this."

Niall began speaking in that guttural language that tree-Fae had used. Either because he had to, or because he wanted to possess someone else, and that had been his reasoning before, right?

At the time, he had already possessed Alistair and there was nothing I could do about it. Now, I wasn't in that boat.

As fast as a snake, I whipped my hand out, pressing two fingers into the smoky mass that masqueraded as a throat. It wasn't solid, but it didn't feel like nothing, either. It was like liquid smoke, and it felt wrong. Not evil, not sordid, but... Wrong. Like he wasn't supposed to be in that form. Like he wasn't supposed to be this way at all. Without much in the way of a spell so much as a thought process and a force of will, I pumped magic into him.

His form flickered a bit, a flash of something pale before it was back to the roiling mass of smoke.

"Try to speak," I ordered, not bothering with niceties.

"I don't know what you think is going to—" Niall muttered. In English. "I can talk! Fates save me, I can talk." He reached to grab me, and a flaming sword was at his throat before I could even blink.

"You would do best to keep your hands to yourself, Niall. No one in this group is going to let you run amuck. Least of all me."

Niall's hands went up in surrender. "Of course, of course. I was just excited. I haven't spoken to a person that wasn't trying to kill me or lead me to my own peril in four centuries. You don't understand what it's like here." He tilted his head back and sighed in relief. "It's like heaven."

"Let's not get off topic, shall we? Lucifer. You knew he was out of his cage. Cough up the details before I drill it out of that smokestack you call a skull."

Niall brought his head back to rights, tilting it down to

stare at me, his odd orange eyes piercing me where I stood. "You wouldn't have come. You wouldn't. Dušan is in danger. I can't fight this fight on my own."

"That isn't giving us details, Niall," I said through gritted teeth. "That is giving me excuses. I don't *want* excuses. I want to know what you know so I can be prepared. Also, I'd like to know whose side you are really fucking on. That would be real good information to have. Just saying."

Niall seemed to wilt in on himself before he folded his limbs and sat on the craggy ground. "I'll tell you, Princess. But you aren't going to like it."

I had no doubt in my mind that statement was true.

I just had no idea how much until it was too late.

CHAPTER TEN

By the time Niall was done with his story, I had not only conjured a bottle of bourbon for myself, but I'd started passing it around. Honestly? There wasn't enough booze in the world to deal with a problem of this magnitude, nor was there a solid solution past "don't die."

"He has been free for four hundred years? Are you fucking kidding me with this bullshit?" Lilith growled for maybe the fifth time before she snatched the decanter out of my hands and started pounding it straight out of the bottle.

Classy, Grandma.

"Well, technically, more than that?" Niall corrected, and personally, I thought it was the way wrong time to do so.

Especially when Lilith's whole body started vibrating with rage. "Then what have I been reinforcing for the last few centuries? A bloody illusion?" she screeched before smashing the decanter on the rocks at her feet.

This was the third bottle she'd thrown, and I was getting tired of conjuring more alcohol. "Would you desist from throwing away good booze? Honestly. And why are you throwing a temper tantrum? This is not a 'temper tantrum' moment. This is a 'devise a plan before the embodiment of evil decides to kill us' moment. Sooooo," I scolded before snapping my fingers in quick succession, "Get the lead out and plan, woman."

"Fuck Soren Quinn. I swear I wish I could rip open the seam, yank his bastard ass out, and kill him all over again. And fuck Abaddon, too. Making that deal. That miserable shit only wanted more power. *More, more, more.* And Samael and Verena. Hell, all the way down to Ruby. If I could resurrect each and every one of them, I would, just so I could kill them myself."

Lilith was a hairsbreadth from losing her mind.

"Well, that's all well and good, dear," Barrett muttered, his tone just a touch snide. "But if you could stop your ranting for a moment, the adults in the room might be able to think of an actual plan. Also, when it is your life's mission to keep an ancient fucking Titan locked away forever, maybe it would be a fabulous idea to, oh, I don't know, *bloody well tell someone*." Barrett started that tirade so calm, but he ended it shouting at the top of his lungs.

Marcus wrapped an arm around Barrett's middle and hauled him back because he was less than a foot from Lilith's face, and that was a deadly place to be. "You losing it is not helping, babe. And quit yelling at Lilith. We all have a blind spot when it comes to family."

Barrett harrumphed in protest.

"We could bring up your parental drama and dissect it for faults if you like."

Barrett narrowed his eyes at his husband, crossing his arms in affront.

"Yes, we all have family drama. None of that explains how we'll keep Grandpa Luci from killing us all. Anyone have a plan for that?" Andras chimed in from his perch on a rather craggy piece of stone. He was pinching his brow like that action alone could stave off the mother of all headaches. Apparently ripping a Fae out of someone's brain hurt.

Who knew?

Okay, I felt a little bad about it, but it was unavoidable.

Probably.

Niall raised his hand like a kindergartener. This was particularly humorous since he was sitting crisscross applesauce in the dirt, his huge mass as foreboding as ever. "I do? Well, it's the same plan I had before. Get

Dušan home safe, make the sacrifice, and let him deal with it?"

Lilith rolled her eyes. "Yes, because that worked out so well before. Dušan refused to kill him. Why do you think he got locked away in the first bloody place?"

Lucifer had many names just like Lilith and Dušan. Lucifer was the god, Cronus, and despite tales to the contrary, he had not, in fact, been killed by Zeus and thrown into Tartarus AKA the Seam.

Locked away, yes. Dead? Not so much. Homer was a lying piece of shit. Good of him to leave out half the damn story let alone the freaking truth.

"Yes, but that was before Lucifer had Verena kill his wife and children," Niall whispered. "Before Dušan was locked away in a pocket world he couldn't get out of for four hundred years. Before Lucifer systematically infiltrated every single part of the world Dušan created, poisoning it. He can't let that stand. *He won't.*"

Niall seemed to have so much hope. So much faith that Dušan would do the right thing. And I wanted to believe him.

I did.

But Lilith brought us all back down to earth.

Lilith snorted. "You think you know my grandfather, but you don't. Lucifer raped Nyx and Dušan did nothing. He flooded the earth, and nothing. He brought wars and destruction to the realms, and nothing. He orchestrated mass genocide, oppression, and misery to all nine realms, *and nothing*. Dušan will do nothing now. He will be silent just like he was when my mother cried at his feet and begged for help."

I wanted to throw up. I wanted to rage. I wanted to…

"He did not do nothing, Lilith, and you know it," Niall countered, and stood for the first time since he began his tale. "Just because he refused to kill his son does not mean he did nothing. Dušan leant his power to the cage. He resurrected the dead—he fixed his son's destruction. And he told you how to lock him away. He told you who could guard the cage. He gave you everything because he couldn't kill Lucifer. Do not lie and say he did nothing. It might have been eons ago, but I was there."

Lilith speared Niall with an expression so scathing it should have set Niall on fire. "Now who is the liar? Hades was the only other person in that room with me, and he's been dead for four hundred years. Abaddon saw to that."

Niall snorted, but took a step back, sitting on a craggy rock next to Andras. The disparity between their two bodies was hilarious. "Not dead, sister. Just stuck in this stupid form, looking for our grandfather and trying not to get myself killed in this absolute travesty of a realm."

At that point I had a thought which my husband voiced aloud. "Is anyone in this bloody realm not a god or goddess? Fates, love, your family tree is fucking bananas. Soon, someone will roll up and say, 'I'm the long-lost son of Apollo' or something, and then we'll all be in trouble."

I wanted to laugh. Really, I did, but I couldn't help but think he was right. Lilith was the daughter of Cronus, Niall was Hades, I was the daughter of Chaos...

"Okay, if anyone else has god lineage, now would be the time to speak up. Seriously, I don't think we can take another one," I called. Yes, I was shouting, but fucking fuck balls, honestly?

Andras raised his hand, "Mine is obvious, but I thought I'd put my hat in the ring so no one is surprised later."

"Not me. My dad is a plain old bastard wraith. Not sure about the mom bit, but I doubt she was a goddess. Then again..." Aidan trailed off. His brother, Ian, was the spawn of their mutual father raping a death goddess, so it wasn't totally out of the realm of possibility for Aidan's mother to be something other than a wraith.

Della was a human before she started out. Alistair was pretty sure he was not of celestial lineage. Barrett and Marcus shook their heads. The only person in question, really, was Zillah and Hideyo. Zillah could not be swayed or influenced by Lucifer. That kinda seemed like a god-like power.

Plus, Zillah's expression was hella guilty. "I don't want to say. You'll look at me weird."

I threw out a guess because, *water dragon*. Duh. "Poseidon? And a dragon?" I may have made a few hand gestures that implied sex, and Zillah blushed all the way up to his hairline.

"I don't know for sure of my mother's name, but she is an ancient. If she's still alive, that is. I've been doing this job a long time. She could be dead by now for all I know."

"But your dad?"

Zillah groaned before parking his ass on a boulder. He seemed ill at ease being out of the water, but I figured that was just because we were in enemy territory. Maybe. "You guessed correct. I don't know him very well, though."

That was messed up, but it made a whole hell of a lot of sense. It seemed a lot of gods didn't feel the need to actually raise their children.

Collectively, the rest of us turned to stare at Hideyo. His eyes widened and he shook his head. "Neither of my parents were a god of any sort. Trust me. If they were, they'd probably still be alive." He said it flippantly, but no amount of sarcasm or sass could hide the pain that leaked into every syllable of that statement.

"Damn," I whispered. "I'm sorry."

He shrugged before looking away. "Yeah, well, this place has always been bloody. Even before Verena."

Damn.

Hideyo had never come out and said he was Fae. Sure, I figured we all knew by now after the not-so-subtle hints that had been dropped, but he'd never said it.

"All of this is well and good, but are we just going to gloss over that you are directly related to Hades?" Alistair griped, staring Lilith down. "Or that your father is running around the Unseelie Court untethered and has been for how long? Or that we need to somehow find Dušan, get him back to the gate, *and* convince him to kill his son in, oh, I don't know…" He trailed off while glancing at his wrist that in no way had a watch on it. "…three bloody days. Less than, if I remember right."

And then, without the least bit of prompting, Alistair stood from his perch on the ottoman I'd conjured and phased. He went from a regal pale-skinned, almost-redhead to a charcoal-skinned devil in an instant. The burning runes carved in his skin glowed like embers, their light brighter with his anger.

"We are losing time. We are losing the element of surprise—if we ever had it—and I will not let you lot put my wife in danger any longer. Get off your asses and let's go. For all we know, Lucifer knows exactly where we are."

None of this was incorrect. Not a single word of it. I almost felt bad for stopping. Almost. Instead of yelling, though, I stood, sidling closer to his rage, and wrapped my arms around his middle. His skin might be made of burning embers, but he was warm, and his heat was welcome. I rested my head on his chest and listened for a heartbeat. It thumped under my ear in a steady clip before it started to slow bit by bit.

There didn't need to be any scolding or yelling. He was right, and now he needed his cool back. The only way we were going to get that was if he got a hug and a deep breath. I was giving the hug. I was still waiting on the deep breath. I gave him until the count of ten before I said something.

"Take a breath, Knight," I whispered, peering up at him. The distance was short, but I still perched my chin on his chest to look him in the eye. "Just one, and then we'll get a move on. You're right, and I'm glad you've taken us to task. One deep breath and we'll go."

Alistair narrowed his eyes before he let his arms surround me, eventually sucking in a huge gulp of air. When he let it out, I saw it all behind his phased eyes. The fear of losing me. The absolute terror at the thought of us not making it.

The loss he was preparing himself for.

I wanted to allay his fears, but they echoed my own. We'd lost a lot. Too much. And this didn't feel like a battle we were going to win.

But damn if we weren't going to try.

CHAPTER ELEVEN

Alistair never got calm enough to phase back to his human form. I didn't blame him. There was little in the way of happy thoughts in a place like this one. Even as calm as I could make myself, thunder still rolled in the distance. I knew without a doubt in my mind that that thunder was mine, and as much as I wanted to project a façade of calm, I was failing pretty miserably at it.

It was possible that it was because Niall—AKA, Hades—was leading us to a mouth of a cave. Maybe it wasn't that it was a cave. Maybe it was that this particular cave resembled a skull. In fact, I wasn't too sure that the rock formation that yawned wide *wasn't* a skull. Out of all the skulls I'd come across—*don't* ask—I could tell it was humanoid with only a slight prominence to the brow. Add in the razor-sharp teeth, and the creep-factor was turned up to eleven. I supposed it was totally possible that someone could have carved that shape out of the rock, but...

I had the sinking suspicion Niall was leading us into the literal mouth of a long-dead beast.

Yeah, calm had waved bye-bye to me somewhere before I fell off the damn cliff and hadn't come back yet.

"There is absolutely no way I am going in that cave," Barrett hissed, and I couldn't help but nod.

In fact, I had to look away from the damn thing because it creeped me out so bad. My gaze fell on the ribbon of a stream we'd been following for the last little bit. And by little bit, I meant hours. The stream we'd been following fell from the mouth of the skull like some kind of macabre tongue snaking through the realm.

Unsettled didn't even cover it. The Unseelie Court was vast, and this trek didn't seem to have an end. The cave was supposed to be a shortcut, but I couldn't see myself taking this path no matter how much time it might save.

"Seconded," Marcus agreed with his husband.

"Thirded," Della chimed in. "Lothan told me about these things. The bones of the old gods—the ones that died to make the new crop. About how the new gods brought down mountains on them, crushing them in the rock. There is no way I'm traipsing around the belly of an old god, Hades. I don't care how much time it will cut off."

Niall huffed, his big body almost wilting at our refusal to go into the cave. Granted, it would cut more than a day off our trek, and the Unseelie castle was still almost half a day away with the shortcut. We did need to save time, but no one—and I mean no one—trusted Niall.

I hated to think it was because he looked like an evil smoke monster, but it wasn't exactly a stretch of the imagination, either. It was also possible it was because he kept a veritable shit-ton of information from us and hid what he was. That wasn't even getting into the whole "possession of two of our people" thing. Yeah… that could be it.

"I can't make you go into the cave. I can't make you do what you said you would. All I can do is…" He trailed off, likely at a loss. "I can't think of what else I'm supposed to do. I spent my whole life serving my grandfather. I sacrificed everything so this realm was better. So that this realm was what my brothers could not make on Earth. That there was very little war, that there was peace. But I failed Dušan, and I'm stuck like this."

Because Niall was a giant smoke monster, it was tough to discern his features unless he made them prominent. But right then, I could almost catch a glimpse of who he used to be, and all of that culminated into a deity that was so sad, so alone, he would risk anything to change it.

I wanted to say something, but Niall continued, "My father is the worst being imaginable. Some of the stories are even true about him. Not all of his children survived. Many of us did not. He did not care. In fact, I think he reveled in it. He won't—he can't—stay in power here. He can't open the gates to Tartarus. And that is exactly what will happen when Faerie collapses, you know? The gate? The one that separates Hell from Faerie? That will crumble to dust. All the Fae doors, all the pockets of worlds, all of the seams holding the realms together. All of it will be gone, leaving the doors wide open for him to walk right on through. Lucifer will rule it all. We don't have the luxury of stopping. We don't have the luxury of time. So, stay out here and walk around the bloody mountain if you want to. Take your time and perish right along with this world. I'm going to get my grandfather. Do what you want."

I felt like I'd been slapped right in the face. Here I was thinking it would just be Faerie that went. And that was bad enough. But Lucifer with a freebie pass to the rest of the realms? Hell's gates open wide with no one strong enough to stop him?

Yep, that was the kick in the ass I needed.

"Welp, can't argue with that," I quipped and moved to follow Niall. Or Hades. Or whatever the fuck we were calling him now. This two-name shit was confusing. I was halted not a second later by Alistair's hand on my elbow. His brow was creased in worry, or maybe it was anger. Maybe it was both. His charred appearance did not lend itself to too many expressions.

"How do we know he's telling the truth, love?" Alistair asked under his breath, and I could feel the trepidation in him calling to me.

Fates, I wanted to comfort him, but I couldn't. I couldn't do anything else but tell him the truth. I sighed, the doubt in me almost too much to bear. "We don't. But I'd rather follow him and kill him later if he's lying than ignore him and let the universe implode. It's a failing of mine, sure, but I figure we can work on it at a later date… yanno, when the world isn't ending. Sound good?"

Alistair growled low and long, his eyes blazing for one tense moment. "Fine. But I expect his death to be bloody and brutal if this is a trap."

It figured that my Knight wasn't going to lose his demon ways anytime soon. I kinda loved that about him. I, too, thirsted for vengeance. What a pair we made.

"So noted." I planted a kiss on his phased lips. The texture of his skin reminded me of brittle stone, but I didn't care. Alistair needed to know that I was in this shit with him. Together, the pair of us followed Niall closer to the mouth of the cave. *Mouth.* Pun totally intended.

Lilith copied Alistair and growled under her breath,

stomping behind us. With much grumbling, the rest of our party followed. They weren't happy about it, but they did it. Hell, I wasn't happy about it, either—especially the closer we got to the fanged teeth that made the entrance. Barrett was the most vocal about it, and it was a comfort to me that his bitching would persevere.

The only person who seemed less and less trusting was Zillah. I couldn't blame him for it, either. He'd been caged for eons and probably wasn't looking to get dead before he'd had a chance to actually live.

I felt a shiver on the wind before I ever heard the rumble. It was like the wind was trying to get my attention this whole damn time, but I was just too stupid to realize it. In fact, I'd thought it was the thunder that had been roiling in the distance since I got to this side of Faerie. But when the earth began to shake, and the stream that carved its way through the land began to rise, I knew that this was totally not me.

Water poured from the mouth of the cave in a rush before drawing down to a trickle, and still, the level of the stream rose. I—along with the majority of our group—whipped my head back in the direction we'd come from, searching for whatever it was that was causing the disturbance.

It took far too long for my brain to cobble together what I was seeing. The water was rising all right. In a wave that crested at least fifty feet high, the water changed shape, morphing into a kind of serpent. The dripping jaws opened wide with surprisingly sharp-looking teeth for a thing made entirely out of water. The thing let out an unearthly screech as it barreled closer, translucent as rippling glass except for a pair of glowing red eyes. My brain snagged on the fact that that noise shouldn't be possible, nor should it be able to come out of a being with no freaking vocal cords.

I knew firsthand what damage water could do. I'd been drowned in a lake a few centuries ago, and it was one of my least favorite ways to go—especially since I'd just barely survived a watery grave. And while I should totally be thinking of how to kill this thing, I was still stuck on the memory of my breath burning in my lungs.

How in the high holy hell were we supposed to fight this thing? It looked like fucking water. Were we supposed to talk to it? Be diplomatic?

Alistair took the choice right out of my hands because he yanked on my arm, and yelled, "Run!"

Yep. Alistair had a way better plan than I did.

Pulling me into the mouth of the cave, his hesitation over this particular path was long gone. The tunnel was black as pitch, the light of the Unseelie Court failing to reach us in this pit. It wasn't until I'd tripped over what I *hoped* were rocks did I toss up a ball of light.

"*Detrahet me in lucem*," I yelled, volleying the light in my hand in the air where it stayed, illuminating our way. Without much time to assess our surroundings, I still caught sight of the spine and rib bones of a giant long-dead creature as we slogged through a rapidly rising stream.

Yup, we were running for our lives from one monster into the belly of another. 'Cause there was no way *that* could go wrong.

Alistair and I were at the back of our little group, so we were within spitting distance of the creature—water monster? Thing?—that was hell-bent on devouring us whole. Though, I didn't see how exactly it was going to do it with water for teeth and no stomach.

I was just absolutely sure it was going to do its damnedest to try. Water rose higher up my legs as we ran, adding to my panic as I tried to keep my feet as the water did its best to trip us. The monster was right behind us, and I didn't think I had time to wield any sort of magic before it would be on me. And I didn't want to find out what would happen when it finally sank its water teeth into us.

And I was so worried about the damn water monster and its glowing red eyes at my back, I wasn't paying any attention to what was in front of us until Alistair and I slammed into the back of Della and Hideyo.

It was as if we froze for a second, balancing precariously on the precipice of what I hoped was a cliff but was more than likely *not*. Then we were falling—or rather *sliding*—hurtling toward the belly of whatever long-dead beast we were stuck inside.

Personally, I would have rather dealt with the damn water monster.

CHAPTER TWELVE

One would think sliding down the spine of a giant skeleton would be sort of fun, right? I mean, slides were always fun. Unless you didn't mean to slide down that particular slope and were now hurtling toward imminent doom. The ball of light had not followed me down the proverbial rabbit hole, and my panicked brain couldn't decide if not knowing what was coming was a good thing or not.

When the ground finally rose up to meet us, I settled on bad. I landed on who I hoped was Alistair, sprawling awkwardly on a body as I heard a pained "*oof*" when I hit the ground. It took a couple of seconds to get my bearings, the darkness and fall doing nothing for my equilibrium.

"What in the blue bloody Fates is this place, Niall?" Barrett demanded, a light blooming in his palm. It illuminated an expression of absolute loathing. "'I know a short-cut,' he says. 'This will be faster,' he says. Did you actually intend us to fall into this bloody pit, you absolute wanker?"

Barrett was not handling this shit any better than I was. I couldn't say why that was a comfort, but it was.

"Fall? No. But this is the way. There isn't usually water in the cave—or at least there wasn't the last time I was here. And there *were* stairs to get down here, but we missed them when that *thing* chased us."

"Speaking of," Andras piped up from his perch on a slimy rock, a place he appeared to have fallen after his initial slide. He paused before yanking on his left wrist. There was a squelching pop and he winced for a moment before breathing a sigh of relief. "What was that thing?"

A screeching roar sounded above us, punctuating Andras' question. And as far as we'd slid, that sound was a little too close for comfort.

Niall sighed, shaking his head. "I don't know. Don't you think if there was a river monster hanging around the shortcut, I would have told you?"

I snorted at the straight absurdity of that statement, but it was my husband who answered him, his voice a quiet ball of rage. "No. Honestly, I think you would have kept us in the dark as long as you possibly could have to ensure the outcome you wanted. Which is what you've done this whole bloody time." Alistair was already phased, but in the low light, his runes glowed with the fire in his blood. "Is there anything else we should be on the lookout for, Niall? Cave dwellers? Stomach monsters?"

Niall growled long and low at him in response but managed to speak a single coherent sentence that was all threat, even though it was not likely intended as one. "I am not your enemy."

"Well, mate, if this is how you treat your friends, I'd hate to see how you treat people you actually dislike."

Antagonistic as fuck, but the statement was still true.

"All right, boys, none of this is getting us closer to our goal. I'd like to get a move on before that damn thing figures out how to get down here." Leave it to my mom to get everyone back on task.

Teresa muttered a few words in Latin and clapped her hands together. Light bloomed bright between her palms, and when she threw her hands wide, dancing bits of light floated from her fingers to cling to the cave ceiling. It was a gifted bit of magic, a simple spell I'd seen her do a thousand times in my youth, made fantastical because of the showmanship. The bits of light cast an eerie green glow in the cave, making what was already a creepy place that much more sinister.

The water monster picked that particular time to roar again. I didn't know if it was just the cave or if my ears were playing tricks on me, but that thing sounded a whole hell of a lot closer than it did a minute ago.

"We need to move. *Now*," I ordered, but I didn't really need to. Anyone who was still putting themselves to rights was up and getting their shit sorted.

Our clip was in no way slow as we followed Niall further into the cave. In fact, I was practically jogging over craggy stones and slimy things to keep up with the group. My mother's spell hovered over our heads, keeping pace with us as we traversed the winding tunnel. And that's the best I could call it. There was nothing special about this particular bit of earth. No pretty crystals, no runes, or carvings. Nothing but bits of rock and slick stones.

Granted, we were in the belly of a long-dead being that in all likelihood could be a god. Why would there be pretty crystals or cave drawings in here? If people were smart, they'd stay as far away from this place as they could get. We—like the idiots we were—thundered through the tunnel, following Niall as he led us deeper and deeper into the earth. The air got cooler and wetter, the moisture in the air clinging to my face and hands, hell, even my hair. And the deeper we got, the less I felt like this was the way to go.

I didn't want to be the whiner of the group, but I was super tempted to ask if we were there yet. I didn't, though, but maybe I should have. Maybe if I would have asked something—*anything*—we might have stopped.

We might have heard the quiet shuffle of footsteps creeping closer in those tiny bits of silence afforded to us between the water monster's roars.

And maybe, just maybe, we wouldn't have been slowly surrounded by what had to be dark elves.

I used the term dark elves very loosely. They did not have dark skin or hair. In fact, they fell into more of the albino spectrum with white skin and hair, their red eyes glowing in the dark. They had the same bone structure as the other elves we'd met, and that was the only reason I would even classify these dark creatures as elves in the first place. Alistair was light years past tense, and I knew he could feel the frisson on the air that told of the elves that crept up from behind us.

I wanted to be diplomatic. We were in their home, stomping around after all. It wasn't cool to just bust down the door to a joint that wasn't yours and start blasting magic. Crown or not, that was just not done. Okay, so it was totally done, it just wasn't going to be done by me.

Alistair tried to stop me by yanking on my hand, but I yanked him right back, pulling him behind me as I weaved through our people to talk to what had to be their leader.

The only reason I thought this dude was the leader was because he had a crown of—*gag*—teeth circling his head like some kind of macabre headband. Add that to the bones hanging from leather thongs at his belt, the still-bloody skin stitched together to make his clothing, and… was that fresh scalps on his belt?

"We mean you no harm or disrespect. We wish to leave this place without violence." I was pretty sure more flowery words were needed, but it was the best I could do under the circumstances. I mean, the guy had fucking scalps hanging from his belt and teeth for a crown. You couldn't be one of the good guys with that much murder on your belt.

"That'sss funny. You breathing is disssressspect," the elf hissed like a snake, his head moving in those sinuous yet jerky movements of a serpent about to strike. "The firssst one to bring me her head will have all the favor you desssire."

Okay, so the diplomatic approach was out. At that moment I should have felt fear. We didn't know how many of them there were. We didn't know where they were coming from or how to get out. One could assume the way out was past Mr. Snaky McTeethcrown, but that wasn't a given.

What *was* a given was the fight we were about to have on our hands.

I think I was looking for that little bit of permission because I didn't hesitate to clap my hands together, unleashing my power in a wave. A fan of lightning sprang from my fingertips, hitting several of the elves in the chest —all except the leader who'd anticipated my actions. He blocked the bolt with a wide sword, the edges and tip jagged as if he'd pulled it from the earth just that way. The metal glowed blue for a short moment, and then he flung the lightning back at me.

I dodged the bolt, yanking Alistair down with me as it arced over our heads. The electricity slammed into an elf that had overtaken Barrett, and the ancient witch shoved the elf off as he writhed. There was a bellowing roar from behind, and as one, the elves converged on us. In close quarters, magic sailed around us—balls of lightning-laced fire from my mother, red arcs of magic from Barrett, my own magics, but it was Lilith's that was the real show-stopper. Icy-white bolts of power found their way to the eyes of our opponents, their consistency as solid as knives as they buried themselves into dark elf brains.

An elf sailed past Alistair's defenses—which were formidable since he was slashing at anything he could reach with his flaming scythe while keeping me behind him—burying his fetid teeth into my shoulder. An enraged growl was ripped from my throat as I latched onto the elf's head and twisted, snapping his neck before throwing him off of me.

But more and more elves came. We were in a sea of

bodies, all fighting in close quarters while trying not to harm our own side. Well, our little pocket of twelve were doing their best. The elves had no compunction about harming their own. A fact proven when their leader rained down bolts of electricity on us. I was hit by one before I managed to throw up a makeshift sort of shield, but it barely held up against the onslaught.

"Max!" Lilith screamed, and I turned toward her voice to watch her hack at an elf with a sword she'd conjured. She cut down elf after elf as I struggled to hold up against the dark elf leader's bombardment. "When he slows, take my hand. We must—"

Lilith's words were cut off as another wave of elves pressed into us, and she didn't explain after that. She dove for my hand, latching onto it as a jolt of power flowed from her into me. It gave me the strength to shove at the leader's onslaught, his power snapping like a dry twig at the flex.

"Everyone!" she called, but it was inside our minds and not out loud. "Take cover." The command rang inside my head before another surge of power hit me. This time, it flowed out of me in a mindless wave. I was merely a conduit for Lilith, hers mingling with mine before it poured out of me.

The earth pitched beneath me, but I was no longer on the ground. My feet hovered over the roiling cave floor as a scream was ripped from my lips. Golden light nearly blinded me as it whipped from my chest, from my skin, from my hands and feet and mouth. As soon as the light touched a dark elf, it seared through their flesh leaving nothing but ashes.

This lasted for far too many too-long moments, and when it died, the walls of the cave shuddered, and then the walls caved in on us.

CHAPTER THIRTEEN

Coming to under a mound of crushing razor-sharp rocks was decidedly my least favorite way to return to consciousness. It was dark, a pitch blackness only reserved for the very pits of Hell. The Seam was brighter than here, and that was saying something. I tried to draw on the earth—hell, I was surrounded by it, might as well use it to my advantage—but the element did not answer me.

I struggled, the first faint strains of claustrophobia setting in as I fought to move. A particularly jagged bit of rock gouged into my side, and every time I jerked, it dug further into my flesh. Panic came fast, and it wasn't until I heard someone else whimper, did I scrap my shit together in the tattered brown paper sack that was my brain.

The earth was not responding because this was not

earth exactly. It was the decaying body of a god or goddess. Meaning that it was possible that the element would be dormant here just like it was near Aiyana and her stupid tree.

The elements are not your only powers, Max. My brain supplied that thought, and if I could have slapped my forehead, I would have.

I breathed a few words in Latin, and the rocks closest to me wiggled. I heard a few rocks topple somewhere above me, but that was about it. After what Lilith did to me—*through me*—I was about as strong as a day-old kitten. My breaths came in shuddered pants, and I did everything I could to not start screaming like a lunatic. This was what I'd always feared—being trapped in the dark, unable to move or escape. This was like every single time I'd died. Stuck in a never-ending thrall of blackness.

Help me. Help me. Fates, please I can't get out. Someone, please, help me.

I didn't know if I just thought those words or screamed them, but my throat was raw and aching, so I probably knew the answer to that. It wasn't until I felt the wash of cool air, did I snap out of what was likely the mother of all panic attacks. It wasn't just cool; it was an icy blast of almost slithering air. If I could have seen anything at all, I had a feeling it would have looked like smoke.

The frigid air hardened, solidifying into the shape of a

man? Niall. Pressure and weight lifted off of me as he took shape, creating space between my prison and my body.

"Shh, child. I'll get you out. Don't fret, dear. You'll see your family again. You'll see them all again. Shh."

It wasn't until I heard Niall's smooth voice, did I realize I had been screaming. Still. After this I was going to need a mental health day… or year. Or decade.

Niall's arm looped around my middle and tugged, pulling me out from under the rocks and debris. Well, not pulled out completely, but a large majority of the heaviest boulders had been moved. I shoved off the last few rocks, positively blissful when I reached unencumbered air.

A familiar warm hand found mine, and Alistair pulled me from the pile. I clung to him and him to me. I wanted to take the time to look him over—check him for injuries —but I didn't. He, on the contrary, ran his hands all over me to assess if I was okay. I knew without his assessment, I had a couple of broken ribs, some bumps and bruises, and probably a concussion. I was a hell of a lot better off than I should be after something like that.

I hurt all over, and yet, I didn't hurt at all because I was with Alistair and he was okay.

"Fates, love. *Fates.* I thought I'd lost you." He pressed a kiss to my forehead but refused to unwrap his arms from my torso. He didn't press on my injured ribs at all, but his arms were an iron cage. I didn't mind. I was shaking like a leaf, leaning on him for support. Only when my eyes focused, did I notice I could see again. It was lighter out from under the rocks, an eerie green glow hovering at the new roof of the cave.

My mother's magic. She was alive. Thank the Fates.

"Who are we missing?" I asked because I didn't see anyone else.

Alistair swiped at his nose—which was bloody and swollen. He had a cut over his right eye and a blooming bruise on his cheek. He'd have a shiner if he didn't heal soon. That said, he seemed better off than I was. "Aidan, Marcus, Hideyo, and Zillah. Niall is looking for them since he can dematerialize with Teresa's help, but Barrett and Teresa can't locate them all. They need your help, love."

Each of those names was like a blow. I took a shuddering breath and touched one of the boulders. The earth was still not talking to me, but I did have other abilities.

"*Invenietis illos,*" I muttered, snapping my fingers. All at once, four balls of light bloomed in the cave above mounds of packed rubble, and we took off. I wanted to ask about the dark elves. Wanted to know what happened after I…

What had Lilith done to me? Through me? She'd said she didn't have time to explain, but whatever she'd done had sapped my abilities to a level that had left me damn near helpless.

"Here!" I yelled to no one in particular.

Alistair and I reached the first light and began yanking rocks—Alistair with much more strength and gusto than me. Then it wasn't just the two of us. Barrett gently moved me out of the way as he scrabbled at the stones to locate his husband. Or at least that was what I'd have been doing if my husband was still under a pile of rocks. With all of our help and Niall's assistance, we unearthed Hideyo. He was conscious and mobile, but he was holding himself funny. Likely he had a dislocated shoulder or maybe a broken collar bone. I couldn't tell in the low light.

His injury didn't slow him down at all, and we came to the next mound. After some tricky maneuvering, we found Zillah. He was unconscious, but breathing, his forehead bleeding like a stuck hog. Once he was mostly unearthed, Barrett sprinted to the next light, yanking boulder after boulder off the mound. Half of us went to help as the rest worked on getting Zillah out of his stone prison.

I could practically feel Barrett vibrating with fear.

"Bloody Fates-forsaken elves. Fucking shortcuts, why did he do that? Why did he push me? I swear to everything I find holy if you're dead, I'll pull you from the depths myself. You aren't leaving me. You bloody well aren't." Barrett muttered his litany of curses as he searched for his husband, and I didn't blame him one bit.

Then the pile of rocks began to vibrate before the

mound moved on its own. Niall materialized next to us as we backed off. Just in time, too, because in the next second, there was a giant gray wolf emerging from the mound, and he wasn't gentle about it, either.

Barrett latched onto my hand and yanked—which hurt like a bitch, by the way—pulling me away from the Alpha wolf.

"Marcus?" I asked, before quickly realizing that the wolf in question might have been Marcus' animal, but that animal was in charge now. He growled at me, snapping his jaws near where I once stood. Alistair shifted me behind his back and began herding me toward the rest of our party.

"Get back," Barrett murmured, his low tone likely used to not startle the giant apex predator. "You're safe, my love. No one is going to hurt you. Please give him back to me."

Barrett stepped fully in front of me and Alistair, making sure the wolf saw him and not us.

"Give him back to me," he pleaded with the animal. Marcus' wolf stared at Barrett for a few tense seconds before he nodded. A thick mist of white magic swirled for a moment, and Marcus appeared a second later, gasping on his hands and knees on the rocky cave floor.

Barrett tackled him—possible injuries be damned—and we left them to their moment to search for the last of our party that was unaccounted for. A pit of dread opened wide within me. Aidan could travel, which meant if he hadn't already saved himself, he was either too weak to do it or he wasn't conscious.

I didn't like either of those options.

Aidan had saved my ass on more than a few occasions, pulling me out of more scrapes than I could count. I couldn't lose him. Not here. Not now.

Soon we got help, and it wasn't just Alistair and I yanking rocks away. It was all of us—at least those of us who were conscious, anyway. We found Aidan at the bottom of too many boulders, his arm covering his head. But that arm was obviously broken, the radial bone protruded from the skin as the rest of the arm hung limp. He was breathing, sure, but he had more than just a broken arm. At least one of his legs was broken—if not both of them—and he had more than a few gashes that poured too much blood.

"We have to get him out of here. I can't draw on the elements in this stupid cave," I muttered under my breath, but Alistair heard me.

"Let me try," my mother offered, laying a hand on Aidan. She dug her fingers in the dirt, whispering a healing spell. It did little to slow the blood seeping from his wounds. She shook her head and tried again, stopping when her nose started to bleed. She growled under her breath before she stood, swaying hard once she reached her feet.

"That's the best I can do. You're right. We need to get out of here. Who knows if there are more dark elves lurking around this Fates forsaken cave? I doubt you vaporized them all."

Vaporized? I wanted to ask to be sure, but I could figure it out for myself. Who knew what spell or power Lilith had used me as a conduit for? Speaking of Lilith, where the fuck was she?

"She's tending to Andras and Della," Alistair whispered, and I whipped my head to him. How in the hell did he know that was on my mind?

"Did you just read my mind? Because that is not cool, man. Not at all."

"I read your face, love. Lilith is bound to care for them. They both are her progeny—in one way or another. Trust me, I want a word with that woman, too. She should not have used you like that. You were never made for death magic. I cannot believe she did that to you." Alistair pulled me behind him as we picked toward what I hoped was an exit. If I never saw another cave again it would be too soon.

I was still processing his words when light filtered into the half-collapsed tunnel. It was slow going with unconscious members of the team, and by the time we made it to the mouth of the tunnel I was steaming mad. I barely took in the gray sky or slate-blue water lapping at the rocky shore.

Death. Magic. Death magic. *Death magic?*

I had the strangest urge to slap the shit out of my grandmother when I saw her kneeling over Andras' wounded side. I had half a mind to tackle her into the rocks and pummel her with my fists until she cried uncle.

Instead, I settled on the tried and true: "What the fuck, Lilith?"

Hasty and rude, sure, but I hadn't used her as a conduit for death magics, which was likely fucking up all my other magic. No, I didn't. She did. And I wanted to be all understanding because yeah, we were in dire straits in that damn cave, but honestly? What. The. Fuck.

"Oh, I'm sorry, should I have run down my plan with you and hammer out the details while those bloody elves were gnawing on our flesh? Or maybe you should just say thank you and shut up about it. I saved our lives." Lilith took that time to tie a field dressing on Andras' abdomen before moving to another wound. She wasn't healing him. Maybe she couldn't.

"Or maybe you could use your own fucking body for death magic and leave mine out of it? How'd that be? I can't draw on the earth, Lilith. None of the elements are responding to me. What the fuck did you do?"

"I did what I thought was best, and—" I never got to find out what excuse she was going to give me.

The world seemed to pitch under our feet. I didn't want to, but I looked back at the mouth of the cave.

Death magics or not, we still had an enemy, and it was coming for us.

CHAPTER FOURTEEN

It seemed like a lifetime ago that Striker and I watched sickly pale hands sprout from the ground like daisies. Unfortunately, it took an inordinate amount of time to remember that top-notch event was only yesterday. Or at least I figured it was yesterday. We'd been on this trek long enough for one day to pass into the next no matter what the sun and moon said.

And just like yesterday, these eyeless monsters with their rancid and rotting flesh were too quick. Erupting from the ground, it took me less than a second to fall back, trying desperately to call on the elements that had served me so well the day before.

But unlike my last battle, when I called on the elements to heal me—to fill me even a little—they refused to answer.

Staggering toward Zillah, I heard Hideyo and Della shout for us to fall back. Teresa and Barrett tossed up feeble barrier spells that wouldn't hold the monsters for very long. I didn't have much power, but if I could get him up, it was one less person to carry. One less person to protect. Zillah wasn't on his feet, but he was sitting up, his eyes wide and fixated on the horde spilling out of the ground.

"Fates-forsaken death magic. Bloody fucking Faerie. Of course, this would be the backlash," Lilith muttered to herself as she finished tying the splint on Andras' leg.

I wanted to ask, but we had more pressing problems at the moment. Kinda like getting the fuck out of here.

"We have to get to the water. Those shades won't follow us in the water." Lilith said that like she not only knew what those zombie-like creatures were but knew what to do about them.

And then it dawned on me—death magic. Verena was using death magic when she opened the gate. Those things were borne of death magics.

Zillah was having trouble focusing on my face, so I grabbed his cheeks and made him look at me. "We need to get into the water. Can you shift? Can you carry us?"

He blinked at me; his face so young for a being so old. He inhaled a sharp breath, his eyes gaining just a little bit of focus. "Yes. I can—I can shift."

He shook his head once as if to clear it before he stood. "You have to cover me while I change. I do—I don't know how long it will take. I'm not at my best."

I nodded, not promising him anything. I wanted to, but I couldn't. Anything I promised him right this second would be a lie. Because one thing was clear: I was under no illusions that we would make it out of here. That we would make it off this beach.

Fear leaked out of my pores as I readied myself. Barrett and Teresa's spells wouldn't hold. Nothing short of Aiyana's magicless tree would keep them at bay. Especially if they were called by death magic. I had a feeling the foul sorcery my grandmother had used me for was still coursing through my veins, still roiling beneath my skin. I wanted to think on it a little, but I had trouble focusing on myself, and a bit too busy refusing to let my skin crawl at Zillah's agonized cries. Like Striker the day before, Zillah's change was not sunshine and lollipops. It was a brutal agony of the highest order.

It had to be.

Anything that caused him to make that sound had to be the worst pain in the universe. Instead of letting that sound shake me to my core, I helped the others clear the beach for the giant sea dragon. Andras was a heavy bastard, but he tried to help as he limped along with his splint made out of gnarled driftwood.

"Let me get him, love. Help the others with the shield," Alistair offered, and I passed off my father before adding my magic to the fight.

My mother and Barrett were doing a complex *obice* spell, the barrier like a mesh of magic keeping the beasts at bay. I added my little bit of magic to theirs, solidifying it to something that might give us enough of a head start into the water.

I didn't trust what Lilith said was true—that they wouldn't follow us. I hoped so, but I didn't believe it. These things seemed to be drawn to death magic, and they wouldn't stop. What I wouldn't give for some of Striker's fire right about now.

Too much magic poured out of me as I lent it to the wall, my legs barely holding me up as I kept the eyeless monsters back. But I didn't fall. My mother and Barrett stood by me, holding me up as we all kept our family safe.

"Zillah is in the water, dear. We need to go," my mother whispered in my ear. But was it a whisper? I had a feeling she was probably yelling it at me.

And then I was up and over a shoulder, a shoulder I knew well enough, as my husband hauled me to our makeshift ride across the water. The spell fizzled out almost immediately, the zombie-like things leaping toward us like they'd just heard the starter pistol.

"Take her," Alistair yelled, and I was given to someone as the light around me promptly went out.

"I CAN'T HEAL HER. THE DEATH MAGIC IN HER blood is too potent. I don't know what to do."

My mother was trying to whisper, *I think*, but she was doing a shit job of it. Granted, we were riding on the back of a water dragon, so it wasn't like there was a lot of real estate to have a private conversation. Well, there was, just not too much above water.

I peeled an eye open, my head rocking a solid eight-point-oh on the Richter scale. Dear sweet mother of all that was holy, why did I feel like I'd been run over by a truck? Oh, right, because my grandmother poured death magic into me like a nut job.

"I can hear you," I groaned, realizing belatedly that I was in Alistair's arms as he kept us firmly fastened to Zillah. I studied what he was holding onto and realized someone somehow must have conjured a harness of some kind so we didn't get pitched overboard. "I don't think that magic agrees with me. Let's never use it again, mm-kay?"

"No bloody shit, love. You stopped breathing there for a minute. I am decidedly not a fan." Alistair's face was haggard with worry, the dirt and blood and fear carving deep grooves into his skin. His nose wasn't swollen anymore, so at least he was healing.

I... wasn't. That couldn't be good.

My mind was as fuzzy as cotton candy—only way less nice—and I hurt all over. Yep. Not good at all.

"Is that why my chest feels like someone sat on it?" I asked because it did. It felt way worse than that, actually. My actual heart hurt, like every beat was a struggle, like someone had a fist around it and was squeezing with all their might.

"Your chest feels like that because I am a first-rate asshole and didn't realize what my magic would do to you." My gaze zeroed in on Lilith, who appeared like she was on death's door. I had a feeling I looked about the same. "I thought that if I pushed my magic through you, with as much power as you had, it would strengthen both sides of the coin. I didn't know that it would attack you, too."

Wait. This was Lilith's power? And my body was rejecting it.

"Take it back. If giving it to me caused this, then take it back." It seemed only logical to me. Uncertainty rose in my gut as I watched Lilith's expression morph from sorrow to abject fear.

"I tried," she whispered. "It won't come back to me even though I called for it."

"So, we're just giving up then?" I scolded her, which in hindsight might not have been the best thing, but whatever. If I was about to kick the bucket, then I was going to be as salty as I wanted to be. "You tried once, and even though this poison in my veins is burning me from the inside out, you're ready to throw in the fucking towel? How about, fuck that?"

I wanted to quit, too, but did she see me doing that? No. I hurt all over. *Alllll over.* Everything from my scalp to my toes felt like it had been put through a fucking meat grinder, and *she* was the one who wanted to quit.

In a spurt of energy I so didn't feel, I sat up. Reaching across Zillah's giant body, I latched onto Lilith's forearm, meeting her shocked expression with my steely gaze. "Try again, or so help me I will haunt your ass until the end of time."

Now that I knew it was there, I could almost feel the poison in my veins. The death magics roiled under my skin like snakes, killing my body faster than it could heal itself. I might not have the elements to heal me, but I wasn't powerless. Pushing, shoving at the blackness that yawned wide within me, I gave Lilith back what was hers.

It was like the steel bands around my heart were snapping one by one. Each bit of power I gave back to her released a tiny bit of the biting pressure in my chest. I sucked in a full breath—my first one since the cave-in—

letting the blessed oxygen into my lungs. Air filled me, healing the ravages of Lilith's power. A lightning bolt streaked across the sky, and I could almost feel the deadly yet playful electricity welcome me back. A clap of thunder was all the warning we got before the rain came. Normally, I'd hate being wet, but the droplets hitting my skin were like kisses from the elements.

It was as if they were sentient. As if they missed me. As if they were worried.

I closed my eyes, tilting my head up as each drop healed me bit by bit. I had spent the last four hundred years without these elements—the last four hundred years without them to sustain me—and I couldn't last one day without them now. Hell, less than that. I'd nearly been keeling over after an hour.

Finally opening my eyes, I settled back in the cradle of Alistair's arms. I didn't look at him, but I still pushed healing magic into him. I knew he needed it even if he didn't say. Again, I never took my gaze off of Lilith. She no longer looked like she felt like day-old garbage.

"No more death magic in the Unseelie Court. Noted."

It was a shit apology under the circumstances, but I was trying very hard not to be a shit about it. "Who hasn't healed yet? I can help."

The worst off was Aidan, his body refusing to heal his shattered arm or broken leg. I did the best I could while we were on Zillah, pulling from the air to push life into him. Still, he screamed like I'd branded him when his radial bone went back where it was supposed to go. I had a feeling me drawing on more than one element would have helped more, but it was the best I could do. Nevertheless, he did not wake, and that worried me more than what would happen when we got back on dry land.

Andras and Hideyo had mostly healed on their own, and Zillah had improved quite a bit when he shifted. But we were all a little bit broken, a cobbled-together band of misfit toys going off into the unknown. Not knowing where we were going did not fill me with joy, but if it meant that we weren't being gnawed on by eyeless zombie things, then I was all for it.

"You said those things were shades?" I asked Lilith, my question startling her out of silence.

Out of the two of us, I recovered a sight bit better than she did. Her skin wasn't sallow, but even though she appeared much better, she was still less than tip-top shape. She shook her head, seemingly to clear it, and answered, "Yes. Shades are the result of death magic. Blood magic can also call them. They look different in every realm. It is not something I do lightly—taking life like that. I suppose if I didn't have a consequence, I could have turned into something like my sisters. But Nyx— knowing who my father was—made sure that I would not be able to use that bit of magic without a steep price to pay."

"But we fought those monsters in the crevasse. They were summoned to the gate when Verena opened it. I don't think Nyx put that limitation on just you," I informed Lilith. "No matter what I did, they would not go away. They just kept coming. Are you sure that the water will keep them back?"

Lilith digested my words for a moment, a green cast to her face as she did so. But her next words chilled me to the absolute bone.

"No, I'm not."

CHAPTER FIFTEEN

The sea churned around Zillah's big body. The dragon knifed through the seemingly endless body of water as if he knew where he was going. I supposed he was getting decent directions from our fearless leader. Niall said he could feel Dušan, and I hoped that was true. I hoped he could lead us to my birth father. I hoped this wasn't just a long line of missteps that took us nowhere.

I couldn't say why I wanted to trust Niall. Nothing he had done so far should allow me to trust him, but something about Niall called to me. He was family in a roundabout way. Not that family hadn't done me wrong. They so had. In fact, ninety percent of the shenanigans that had resulted in my utter ruin resulted from familial intervention.

It was official. I was a crazy person. Only a crazy person would be riding on the back of a water dragon as they ran away from shade-zombies on her way to rescue her literal god of a father from the ruler of the Unseelie Court, AKA, the head honcho of evil: Lucifer.

This was the actual definition of bat-shit insane. I chuckled to myself as I shook my head, embracing my insanity. Niall needed my help, and somehow that edged out my trepidation. I didn't know how it did, but it was a little too late to back out now. Especially since I couldn't actually see an end to this body of water.

Niall's smoky form rested at the scant amount of real estate between Zillah's horns. As fast as we were moving, I had no doubt that he had given Zillah a heading. Or maybe—unlike me—they could sense Dušan in this crazy backward place.

I wanted to climb Zillah's back and have a little logistical meeting with the pair of them, but I also wanted to take a tiny bit of a rest that wasn't mandated by involuntary unconsciousness. Plus, a little brainstorming session over what we would do if we actually met up with the literal devil should probably be penciled in at the top of the docket at some point.

I bet each member of my family was kicking themselves for deciding to ambush me at the gate. None of them should have followed me here. And no amount of positivity was going to make me think we were going to get out of this with just the damage we'd already sustained. Aidan was still out, and the longer time passed without him waking, the more worried I got.

I'd decided to try to heal Aidan a little bit more—if I even could—and was untethered for maybe a millisecond when Zillah's big body thrashed. The unholy roar coming from his mouth chilled me to the bone. And that bone-chilling was happening even though I was hurtling toward the churning water. In the next instant, someone snagged my hand, keeping me from falling into what I now knew was monster-infested water.

The monsters themselves were something out of a Lovecraft novel, miniature Leviathan things with needles for teeth like a piranha. And there were thousands of them thrashing in the water as they attacked Zillah.

I was too busy staring at the growing pool of red staining the water to really worry too much about the hand that held me. I knew it was Alistair. I also knew that if he dropped me, I was going to be a monster's dinner.

Zillah let out another unholy roar, one that should have scared these parasites off if they knew what was good for them, but they paid him no mind. Alistair yanked me up onto Zillah's back, fastening something to my waist before he said a single thing to me. Rage painted his face in his fiery runes, his charcoal skin overtaking his human form.

"Help Zillah, love," he yelled before tossing a rope over the side of Zillah's colossal body and jumping after it.

"Alistair!" I screamed, trying to reach him but failing once I'd reached the end of my tether. I could see him, though, and he was hacking near the water with his flaming scythe, trying to knock the monsters away from Zillah's side.

Help Zillah, love.

Okay. I could do that. Crouching on his big back, I shoved my power into the big lug, letting the air and water heal as much as the monsters took. But they were attacking too fast, too much. Zillah's speed and my power couldn't keep up with the damage.

I changed tactics, calling on the water to help. But the water didn't answer me this time, too busy taking the blood offered for itself. A flash fire of rage made my skin prickle, and that was my only warning before lightning rained down on the water, stabbing like knives.

With surgical precision, brilliant blue bolts of lightning speared the Leviathans burning them to ash. The problem was there was not enough lightning in the entire realm to take care of the horde attacking Zillah. We had to get out of the water. There was nothing else I could do. Not unless... Unless I pushed Zillah where I wanted him to be.

As insane as it was, I didn't see a whole lot of other options. Pulling on Zillah, on the elements, on everything in this realm, I pushed, forcing Zillah out of the water, out of the horde, out of it all. All I thought of was land—we needed land.

The push felt like I was ripping myself in two. A sensation that was not wholly unexpected since I was shoving a giant serpent and all the little fleas attached to it through space and time. When we landed with a giant splash in a rocky shallow—so not quite land, but close—I may or may not have vomited on his scales.

Zillah did not notice. He was too busy thrashing, trying to get the last of the Leviathans off of him. Alistair, Andras, and Hideyo jumped in to help, stabbing at the remaining monsters with their blades. Zillah shuddered, thrashed once again, and then began to shrink. His body shifted back to his human form, likely without his consent as unconsciousness pulled at him.

Niall and Lilith were carrying Aidan to shore while Teresa and Barrett were volleying fireballs and inky-purple smoke bombs at the few surviving monsters. The rest of us were doing our level best not to drown in the crashing waves and swift undertow. I knifed through the water, latching onto Zillah's ravaged human form as I hauled us both toward the shore.

Zillah—I could tell without even being out of the water

yet—was in bad shape. Inky-red blood stained the water around us, wafting through the waves like red ink. If we didn't get this bleeding stopped, I didn't know if the kid would survive. And I knew Zillah was older than me by several thousand years, but he looked so young. Stuck in his dragon form so long, he'd likely been arrested at the age he'd made the bargain. Zillah had a teenage-boy build, fine-boned with a hint of the man he'd become—the man he'd become if he made it through this mess.

The rocky beach was mostly black sand interspersed with razor-sharp green glass and gnarled driftwood. I tried to find a clear spot, kicking away a few larger pieces of wood only to realize that they were not wood at all but bones.

I refused to ponder that too hard, focusing on Zillah and what I could do for him. Huge chunks of flesh were ripped from his body, parts of his leg cut all the way down to the bone. He was missing fingers on his left hand. I tried very hard not to look too closely at his injuries as tunnel vision hit me hard.

Unlike when he was being attacked, this time when I called on the water for assistance, it answered, funneling power into Zillah's battered body. But the water only answered for so long, the mercurial element leaving me to patch up the rest of Zillah's injuries on my own.

"Where in the bloody hell are we?" Barrett demanded,

shoving sodden hair off his face as he knelt next to me as we tried to patch Zillah up.

"I have absolutely no idea. All I thought was we needed land. I can't say I deliberated too much on it." I was the queen of not looking before I leapt, but in this one instance, I didn't think I did too bad.

"I'm not complaining," Andras muttered, kneeling next to me and wrapping an arm around my shoulders. "You did good, kid. We need to stop his bleeding and then move. We can't stay on this beach."

I agreed with him even though I didn't say it out loud. There was a hum on the air, a pulse of power raking across my exposed skin. We were too exposed here. Instead of the water—who was being an epic shithead right now—I coaxed the earth into Zillah. Letting the element fill him, I watched as the largest of the injuries repaired themselves. But there was only so much the element could do here in this muted place, so when the bleeding stopped, I did, too, hoping that what I'd done was enough.

It didn't feel like it.

"We need to move," Niall echoed, pulling the injured dragon from the shore.

Andras helped Hideyo with Aidan, and we followed Niall to an outcropping of barren trees. I took in my surroundings for the first time since I'd dropped us in the shallows. The sun was dimmed by a green cast, the sky a gangrenous roiling of clouds. Further up the shore were ruined stone buildings, their roofs caved in some places. A crumbling bridge led to a dark castle, foreboding spires reaching up to the sky like a clawed hand.

If I could pick a place that embodied a *"fuck that"* vibe, this would legit be it. It wasn't cold enough to snow, but little tufts of white fell from the sky—which considering where we were—did not fill me with joy.

Niall led us within the tree line, and I appreciated the little bit of cover. "We have to leave them here," he murmured, setting Zillah down on a bed of slimy leaves and black moss. "The maze is too treacherous. They could die."

"Maze?" Alistair asked, echoing my thoughts.

Niall seemed to nod but did not take his eyes off the wounded dragon. "You took us to the right place, Max. This is the Unseelie Court. But it isn't like we can just break into the castle to find Dušan—if that is even where he is. This whole bloody kingdom is full of booby traps. We have to make it to the castle first."

I was still stuck on *"if that is even where he is"* part of the convo to get too mired in the booby trap portion of that statement. Teresa, though, was on the ball.

"Booby traps? Maze? What is this, *Indiana Jones*? What in the blue fuck did you get us into, Niall?"

"What I want to know," I broke in, interrupting what

was probably going to be a spectacular motherly tirade, "is what do you mean by *'if that is even where he is?'*"

Niall growled at us, and if the man had hair, I was sure he was three seconds away from ripping it out. "I don't know. All I had was a heading, but now that we're here, I feel Dušan everywhere. Don't you? Like a buzz on my flesh. He is here, I feel it. But I don't know where."

That was understandable. I felt that buzz, too, and I told him so. "But a maze?" I asked, wanting to clarify that little nugget of info.

"Lucifer is a grade-A prick and loves to fuck with anyone attempting to access the Court. You had to have seen the bones on the shore. Had I known the maze started in the water, I would have suggested another route. But it's like I can't think in this body anymore. I know I've been here. I know I've seen everything there is to see. I've been trapped on this side of the wall for centuries. I knew this day would come. But everything is so bloody fuzzy." Niall shook his head. "I don't know how much help I will be to you anymore. I don't know if I can find him."

A whimper fell from his mouth, the sound practically gutting me.

I had to do something. Again, without much in the way of forethought, I put my hand on Niall's shoulder. The giant smoke monster was nearly solid to the touch, and he shuddered at the contact. Like I'd done to so many others, I pushed, searching for the thread of whatever it was that held him down, kept him locked up.

The blackened thread of magic was old. Old and fetid. Slowly poisoning him as it tied itself around and around his mind. It reminded me so much of the threads on Cinder, on Striker. It had a similar signature. But Soren was dead, and so was Verena. What had Niall said? Abaddon had done this to him?

And this was a magic that could not be broken by death or time. This was a magic that could only be broken by someone like me. Like so many other spells, I plucked at the oily threads, snapping them one by one.

Even before my glamour was lifted, no one could keep me out. And Abaddon wouldn't be able to, either.

CHAPTER SIXTEEN

Niall did not look like himself. Or maybe now that he was no longer an eight-foot-tall smoke monster, he looked like himself for the first time in four centuries. He was still impossibly tall, but that was about where the similarities ended. Golden hair cascaded down his back in a sheet. And by golden, I did not mean blond. I meant gold. Little flecks of metallic radiance glinted in the low light. His skin was paler than the palest human, without so much as a hint of pink or yellow undertone.

His eyes matched his hair, and although they were eerie in the extreme, the shade also fit him. His nose was like a knife blade, his cheeks sharp like mine, his jaw matching them both. A pair of jagged horns peeked out of his hair, too large to be called dainty and too small to be

152 · ANNIE ANDERSON

foreboding. A thin line of black indented his face from one temple, over his nose to the other temple, a trail of three dots underscoring the curve of his cheeks. His lips were full but held no color, the flesh just as pale as the rest of him. He had dark slashes for eyebrows, the hair in no way matching the rest of him, but somehow it pulled his features together.

He wasn't pretty, nor would I call him handsome, but he was unearthly attractive in a way I couldn't name. The smoke monster was Niall. *This* was Hades.

He stared at his hands for long moments—moments we probably did not have—in awe of his body now returned to him. "You actually did it. I didn't think you would be able to break that spell, but you actually bloody did it."

"Brother," Lilith breathed, pushing between Barrett and Marcus to get to the tall man. She wrapped her arms around his waist and hugged him. "I didn't believe you when you said... Fates, how can you forgive me? I didn't look for you. I thought you were dead. I thought..." Lilith began to sob, and it was the first time I'd ever seen her show that kind of emotion. Bernadette had always been that stiff-upper-lip kind of British woman, even though she was neither British nor the aging grandmother she portrayed herself as.

Andras just blinked at his uncle, his expression blank.

Just like the rest of us, Andras hadn't believed Niall when he told us who he was, hadn't believed him when he said he could feel Dušan calling him.

None of us had believed him at all.

I wanted to apologize to him, but time was of the essence, and it was running out. Plus, in that dark part of myself I so desperately did not like to acknowledge, I was jealous. Lilith had thought her brother was dead. And now, by some weird turn of events, she had him back. I wasn't ever getting Maria back. There was no spell to do, no voyage to traverse. Maria was gone, and as happy as I was that Lilith got her second chance, I was bitter as fuck about not ever getting mine.

Which is probably why I was bitchy as all get out when I said, "I love a family reunion as much as the next gal, but I was under the impression we needed to *not* be caught here. We need to hide Aidan and Zillah and pray no one finds them. The elements are wonky as fuck here and have no desire to help me out. I can't heal them any more than I already have."

Alistair squeezed my hand, and instantly, I felt terrible. Lilith's face fell, and that gutted me more than I'd care to admit. I was an asshole of the highest order.

"I'm sorry," I murmured. "That was a bitchy thing to say, and I'm a dick for ruining your moment. I'm a jealous shitbag."

Lilith didn't give me any shit. Like the grandmother I'd come to rely on this last year, she broke away from her brother and enveloped me in a hug. "You're healing, dear. You can be a jealous shitbag every now again if you need to."

"I'm glad you got your brother back."

"I'm sorry you lost Maria. I'd get her back for you if I could."

"I know. You're awesome like that."

"Okay," Barrett broke in, "this is touching and all that rot, but we are in enemy territory. Maze? Booby traps?" He snapped his fingers like we were supposed to hop to, and I, for one, adored his peeved nature.

"It will be an unfortunate follow-the-leader sort of thing," Hades answered. "There are too many traps to count, and the route is long. The only good thing is I don't believe they are altered too often, so my last foray into this batch of idiocy should provide us with enough information to stay alive. Not getting caught is the name of the game here, boys and girls. And there are plenty of ways to do that."

Hades' speech was less than comforting, but honesty was appreciated, especially here.

"I don't know where Dušan is. He could be in the maze. He could be in the castle. He could be roasting on a spit in Lucifer's kitchen for all I know. So keep your eyes peeled."

I looked down at our wounded. I didn't want to leave them behind, but I didn't see another option. Zillah wasn't going to come to anytime soon, but Aidan seemed to be rousing. As much as we needed to move, I couldn't —we couldn't—without making sure they were protected.

Aidan's bottle-green eyes flashed open, fear filling them as he struggled to sit up. Hideyo and I put a quelling hand on his shoulders. "Easy there, friend. Easy," Hideyo murmured.

"Where are the elves? What happened?" Aidan croaked, and for the first time since we found him unconscious, did I breathe a little sigh of relief.

"Vaporized. You missed the zombie-shades and the piranha sea monsters while you were out."

Aidan's eyes flew wide. "Zombie-shades and piranha sea monsters? What the fuck kind of place is this?"

Alistair huffed from behind me, and I glanced up to see him scanning the tree line for threats. "An offshoot of Hell would be my guess. Bloody Lucifer. How in the Fates-forsaken fuck did he build this much power and hold it under wraps for this long? Do the Fates not care one whit about the rest of us?"

I followed his gaze to the Unseelie Court and its destroyed landscape. He had a point. Lucifer had either built this from scratch—which I thought was unlikely—or he'd taken over someone else's kingdom. The air had the feeling of the downtrodden and long dead. The only thing I could equate it to was the same feeling one got when traversing near the decommissioned concentration camps in Europe. It felt like torture and death and persecution.

If I squinted, I could envision what this place once was —before it became the devil's playground.

But I also knew that the Fates had their hands tied. But who or what, I wasn't sure. Nor was I sure what bargain they made that kept them shackled to silence.

"You and Zillah are hurt," I began, unable to explain the how's or why's. "There is a maze we have to go through, but you aren't well enough to—"

"No," Aidan growled. "Not without me, you're not."

His vehemence made me want to cry. Aidan took his job as a paladin more seriously than I realized.

"It's bad enough you went to Hell without me. I'm not letting you do this, too. Your grandmother would skin me alive if you got hurt."

Lilith huffed. "While under normal circumstances, you'd be right, I can't under good conscience let you go in there. Max will want to save you instead of the other way 'round, and then she'll end up getting hurt because of it. No, my dear boy, staying here and keeping watch over Zillah is a much better plan." Lilith crouched next to

Aidan. "You have done everything I have ever asked of you and more. It is not a shame to do what you must to survive, dear."

Aidan did not appear appeased in the least, but he sat up and put on a brave face.

"We're going to hide you, okay? But you are in charge of Zillah." I knew that if I didn't give Aidan a job to do, he would end up following us, anyway. It was in his nature to protect—to care for someone other than himself. Maybe if he stood watch over Zillah, I wouldn't have to worry about him hobbling through booby traps on his own.

"You're just making me watch him because you don't want me to follow you," he grumbled, guessing our motivations easily enough. "I used to do the same shit to Ian when I wanted him out of the way."

"Oh, get over it. You're hurt, and Zillah is unconscious," Della griped, totally done with Aidan's bullshit. "We can't carry him and worry about you, too. Watch over the man who carried your ass on his back to safety and quit bitching about it." The vampire was showing quite a bit of fang, and I didn't blame her one bit. This shit was stressful.

Properly chastised by Della's epic "Mom voice," Aidan snapped his mouth shut, giving her a nod. "Fine, but everyone better come out of there or else."

I wanted to smile at his empty threat, but I couldn't. There was too much at risk, too much to lose if we failed.

"We'll do our best," I muttered, unable to lie even in this. "Now sit still. I need to ward you two against harm. If you ever feel up to it, try and travel out of here. Take Zillah home with you. Don't leave him to this place. He deserves a life." *And so do you,* I thought, trying not to make this sound like a goodbye. Aidan had sacrificed his whole life for someone else. Protecting his brother, in service to a king, trying to keep me from dying for the thousandth time. If he made it out of here and I didn't, he needed to live.

"Don't push it, Max," was all he said back, and I had a feeling that was the best I was going to get.

Without anything better to say, I began my wards, offering protection and concealment, and health. When I was done, Teresa added to them. When she finished hers, Barrett added to them both.

Unable to voice just how much I did not like leaving him to the dangers in this rotten place, I got up, walking away from one of the few people in this universe who hadn't yet let me down.

"Stay safe, mate," Alistair murmured before joining me, and the pair of us stared at the crumbling city at the base of the castle. That would be our maze, our obstacle. For a split second, I wanted to cry. Here I was about to head into the unknown, and as mad and scared as I was, I was glad Alistair was here with me.

How fucking selfish did that make me?

"Stop it," Alistair scolded, and I really had to wonder if he could read my mind.

"You really are going to have to tell me if you have somehow turned telepathic. It's rude not to, you know."

Instead of answering me, he pressed a kiss to my mouth. And not a quick one, either. It was slow and full of promise. It felt like a promise for a future, and I so wanted that with him. "Not telepathic, love," he finally answered when we came up for air. "But you had that guilty look on your face like you wanted something you knew you shouldn't have. We can't know what is waiting for us, love, but I'd rather be at your side fighting with you than knowing you were off on your own any day of the week. Don't regret me being here, because I wouldn't have it any other way."

I wanted to joke, but I just didn't have it in me. Instead, I told him I loved him, because who knew how many more times in this life I would get to. "I love you to the ends of the earth and far beyond. Vaster than Heaven or Hell or any of the worlds in between."

And I'll do that in this life or the next.

I thought it but didn't say it. Still, I figured he heard me.

CHAPTER SEVENTEEN

H ades informed us that there were several paths into the maze as well as several exits. I found that fact comforting, even though it offered a high probability that we would get lost. Mazes meant we could get out. Labyrinths were a whole other story. The absolute last thing we needed was a labyrinth with only one entrance that led us to the middle of who knew what.

Hades led us to a nearly blocked off entrance close to the copse of trees where we left Aidan and Zillah. It was hard to gauge how far we would need to travel, and no one wanted to think about what we would need to do while we were in that maze. It was possible Dušan was stuck in there somewhere, but I didn't think we would be that lucky. What were the odds an immortal being with eons of life would get tripped up by a damn maze?

Us? I could totally see that happening.

This path was bisected by a fallen stone monolith, the crumbling rock blocking half of the entrance. As soon as we crossed what I considered the threshold of the maze, the biting power that had raked my skin since we'd gotten here sizzled against my flesh. I hissed at the pain, but shook my head when Alistair gave me a questioning look. If what Hades said was true, then this was Dušan's signature. Or at least I hoped this was him. If it wasn't, then we had a whole host of other problems.

The maze walls were higher than fifty feet, and as craggy and pitted as they were, they seemed too steep to climb. It wasn't like we could just scale to the top and walk this bitch. No, this would have to be done the old-fashioned way.

I just hoped Hades remembered the damned path.

The maze floor was littered with bones and other unsavory things. Like ruined armor and broken weapons. Whatever obstacle or trap that had been here before did not seem to be here now. Not that I was complaining, but it did fill me with a sense of dread as we waited for the other shoe to drop. It was too quiet here—the only sound was our shuffling feet as we carefully stepped where Hades told us to. In Faerie proper, there was always a bird cawing or a babbling brook or *something*. Here in this little pit of doom? Nada.

The earth vibrated under our feet, nothing like what I did when I was mad, more like the concussion that radiated outward when an elephant stomped. A looming shadow fell over us, and I stared *up, up, up* to find the biggest creature I'd ever seen resting his shoulder against one of the maze walls. Easily twenty feet tall, the giant wore a sleeveless tunic and breeches, and other than the bands around his wrists and ankles, he wore nothing else.

No shoes, no belt, no weapons. Which I supposed was good since if this guy had a weapon it would have to be enormous, and we would be ten times more screwed than we currently were. Shaggy haired with an unkempt beard, the man's face boasted only one eye at the center of his forehead, with two divots in his face where his other eyes should be but weren't. A single eye that locked gazes with me and refused to blink. Well, I was so small in comparison that he could be looking at any one of us, but I had a feeling he was looking at just me.

I should have felt a healthy amount of fear—I mean, this was a fucking cyclops—but something inside me whispered that this giant was not a threat exactly. Greek mythology told of three different types of cyclops. The imprisoned children of Gaia, the Homeric ones that were raving monsters, and the wall builders. Since Homer had

164 · ANNIE ANDERSON

been full of shit in regard to Cronus, AKA Lucifer, I had little in the way of faith that any of his other bullshit tales were true.

And that was probably why I stayed where I was when my other compatriots decided to try and rush the giant. Andras attacked first, his smoky demon body all talons and teeth as he raced toward the cyclops. He didn't make it very far, though. With a bored flick of his hand, the cyclops flung Andras back to us, his smoky body phasing back to his human one when he landed in a heap.

Then the rest attacked at once—well, Hades, Lilith, and I didn't. Hades and Lilith just stood there, not lifting a finger or saying a damn word. Hades, the sod, had a little smile playing at the corners of his mouth.

I rolled my eyes and snapped my fingers, transporting myself in front of my family. The group as a whole took a few seconds to skid to a stop.

"What the fuck, Max?" Barrett scolded, the purple-red magic on his palms fizzling out. The rest of them seemed to share his sentiment, but I answered Barrett all the same.

"What the fuck, what? Has this man attacked you in any way? Has he done anything but defend himself? Do you see Hades or Lilith attacking? No. I don't know what kind of bullshit game this is, but attacking is not the answer, so..." I turned my back to my family and craned my neck so I could stare at the giant. "What do you want?"

"You're no fun, you know that?" the cyclops muttered before plopping down in the middle of the path. And when this dude plopped, the whole of the earth shook. It was similar to when I made the earth pitch, and I barely kept my balance.

"So I've been told. You got a name, dude?" I sighed, pinching the skin between my brows. This was going to be a riddle or a bargain, I could just feel it.

"Argus," he answered, seemingly pleased I asked. Argus was one of the three cyclops that made Zeus' thunderbolts. Or at least that was the way Hesiod told it. Who knew how much of that was bullshit?

"Okay, Argus, I would like to go past you so I can get my father back. Are you going to let us pass?" Yes, my tone was exasperated as fuck, but come on. Unless I bargained my ass off, we weren't getting past this guy. Like ever.

Argus put on a show of tapping his bottom lip as he pretended to ponder something. It was ripely overdone and dramatic. Who knew cyclopes were such bad actors? Not me, that's for sure. Granted, I didn't think about cyclopes in general, so I couldn't judge.

"Maybe," Argus said in a sing-song voice, which was disconcerting as hell because no man who was that big and that menacing should ever sing-song anything. Ever. "But maybe not. You did take all the fun out of smiting you all. No one ever comes to visit me anymore. How am I supposed to enjoy myself if I don't get to squash people?"

I wanted to roll my eyes, but I managed not to. Argus was acting like he was a third grader reading from a shitty script. "Have you tried knitting? I've heard that's a cool hobby. Plus, if I don't find Dušan, then it won't really matter, now will it? This little slice of Faerie will all go poof, and you probably with it."

Argus' face lit up at my joke, but his frown was real when I mentioned I was Dušan's daughter. "A daughter of Chaos? You shouldn't be here."

I shrugged. "No shit. I should be on a beach sipping booze from an umbrella drink and enjoying my honeymoon. Instead, I have to stop a civil war, an apocalypse, and rescue my father all at the same time. I'm tired. I'm cranky. I want this over with so I can go sleep for a decade or three, but I can't until you. Move. Out. Of. My. Way. So, what's it gonna be? You want something, so spit it out."

Argus regarded me for a long moment. "I lost my brothers because I would not give myself over to Cronus. Because I would not bargain with him. He killed them in front of me as punishment for the cell we made. To further twist the knife, before he killed them, he made me create these manacles. He said he would spare my brothers if I made them, wore them, and remanded myself to this maze." He gestured to the bands around his wrists and ankles. "They keep me here. Unable to leave. Unable to die. Unable to hide. And then he killed them anyway. You lost your sister. You understand my rage."

How he knew I lost Maria was anyone's guess, but it didn't matter.

"Here is my bargain, daughter of Chaos. Remove my bonds, and I will step out of your way. Don't, and we'll both sit here until this world is no more."

A freebie pass through the maze in exchange for removing a man from bondage? No contest. I would gladly remove those manacles if it meant he would be free.

Just like me, he'd earned it.

But I wasn't a sucker either, so I made sure to clarify. Alistair had taught me that the devil really was in the details after all. "And by step out of my way, you mean what? I think I'm going to need some details, bud."

Argus' smile was damn near boyish. He was absolutely delighted that I called him on this little bit of almost deception.

"How about this," I offered, "I remove your bonds as best as I am able, and you step aside and let us through the maze. You may not harm anyone in my party, nor may you inform anyone that we're here." I paused to turn to Alistair, "Did I forget anything?"

"You might want to add a caveat that he cannot impede us when we exit the maze, nor lie in wait for us to murder us after we exit. Just to cover all the bases."

I turned back to Argus. "What he said. Deal?"

"A goddess married to a demon? I wonder what your father thinks about that," Argus remarked as if he had all the time in the world. Wasn't this the same guy who wanted to burn this bitch to the ground two seconds ago?

"He likes my husband just fine, thank you. And what does that have to do with anything? Quit stalling. Do we have a deal or not?"

Argus stared at me for a long second, his lone eye piercing me where I stood. What? I had a limited amount of time and he was wasting it. "You are very rude, daughter of Chaos."

"And you're wasting my fucking time. I have until the Blood Moon to get Dušan back or else Faerie goes bye-bye. What about that time constraint is lost on you? Do we have a deal?" I repeated, you know, just in case he fucking forgot what we were doing here. Did he not want his bonds off or what?

I was super tempted to just snap my way around him, but I was hesitant to do that after the whole bridge incident. Who knew what was behind his giant body or what kind of traps were just chilling back there? I knew I was going to find out soon enough, but still, I didn't want to trip one if I didn't have to.

"You've played enough, Argus," Hades called as he sidled up next to me. "Stop torturing her and complete the bargain. Time is of the essence."

Even with the backup, I wanted to smash something. It shouldn't take Hades' intervention to get Argus to make the deal he'd specifically requested—even if it did have a few caveats.

"But it means I can't play with them when they're through. How am I supposed to have any fun if I can't try and ambush them later?"

I blinked, blinked again, and then completely lost the very last shred of my mind. Snapping my fingers, I shoved Argus up to his feet and pressed him against the giant wall. I wasn't a hundred percent sure what I'd put into that spell, but I was for damn certain he wasn't going to be able to move anytime soon. A few weeks ago, I'd had trouble lifting a single wolf, now I was just pissed enough to move a whole fucking giant. Granted, that was before my glamour was gone, but still. I was kind of proud of myself.

"You could have had your bonds off if you were actually willing to deal. Now you get nothing," I scolded Argus, readily admitting to myself that I had just likely made an enemy.

Did I care at that point? Absolutely not.

Would I care later? Probably.

"When you decide to get your head out of your ass, come find me and I'll help you. Until then, Argus, I want you to think long and hard about how much your *fun* is worth." I turned to the slack-jawed group of people behind me. "Let's go."

Out of all of them, the only ones who were not even a little surprised at my antics were Alistair, Barrett, and my mother. In fact, Teresa and Barrett were trying their level best not to start laughing.

Hades was miraculously paler than he had been moments earlier—a feat I didn't think was possible—his mouth open wide in shock. "How? Bu—*how*?"

Barrett snickered before slapping him on the shoulder. "First time? No worries, mate, you'll get used to it. How about you lead on then?"

Barrett guided Hades past Argus, and the rest followed them. I stayed back to impart one last thing to the cyclops. "I am not an enemy. When you come for me—and I know you will—remember that."

With that said, I brushed past him, releasing him from his confines as I went.

But he didn't come after us, and he didn't say another word. I couldn't tell if that was a good thing or not.

With my luck? I was likely in for a world of hurt.

CHAPTER EIGHTEEN

Hades was still stunned at my exchange with Argus by the time we'd rounded the second and third turns in the maze, which I supposed I didn't blame him for. Still, he needed to get his head in the game before we accidentally stepped on Faerie's version of a land mine and blew ourselves to kingdom come. We arrived at a weird three-pronged fork in the path. One way seemed to go below ground, the other went up, and the third stayed the course. All three seemed to be sucky options, but Hades was giving us nothing.

He just stood there and blinked, his shock getting the better of him.

"Okay, Obi Wan, wanna tell us which way we're supposed to go?" I quipped. I'd practically skipped when I came back to the group, but the longer we walked the less joy I felt. It was probably a bad thing that I felt a sense of satisfaction at pinning Argus to the wall. I mean, he was stuck here against his will and had watched his brothers die. Then again, if I had watched Lucifer kill my sister, it was unlikely that I would be dragging my feet on the deal that would free me to take him out, so there was that.

"Obi Wan?" he finally answered.

I shook my head. "*Star Wars* reference. Unless you're up on your pop culture, you won't get it."

"Pop culture?"

"Popular culture. What the kids are saying these days? Never mind. What I mean is, do you want to get over your shock and get to the leading portion of our endeavor? Is that clear enough?"

Hades' stunned expression didn't waver. "But you just picked him up and shoved him against the wall."

Ah. So he was still stuck on that.

"She also lifted a giant water dragon out of Siren-infested water and saved us all. How are you confused about the cyclops and not that?" Teresa quipped, and I had to hold back a snort. Leave it to my mother to get to the meat of the issue.

Hades' face paled. "You're right. How did you do that?"

I shrugged and shook my head. "I don't know, man, I just work here. Time crunch? Dušan? Can we go?"

It was a little disconcerting that my display of power was shocking. I mean, I thought he needed my help. Wasn't that what he said? That he needed me to find Dušan. He needed me to do this job. If he needed me so bad, wasn't it a good thing that I was coming through for him in a clutch?

"But you are a demigod. Not a goddess. How are you able to do all this? I was there the day you were born. I knew your mother. I—" He shook his head. "Those are not demigod powers, Massima."

A shrug was as best as I could come up with. "When we find Dušan, you can ask him. He would know better than I would. For now, I'm just trying not to be an asshole about the powers I do have, and that's about all I can do. Now, that path?" I pointed to the one that went up. The castle itself was on a higher elevation than where we were currently standing, so it sort of made sense, but I couldn't be sure in a place like this.

Hades shook his head, gesturing to the path that went below ground, the path lit by unearthly blue torches that seemed to be fueled by magic alone. "That is the way, but follow my feet. One wrong step will bring you a world of pain." He shuddered at the thought, and I figured it was best not to ask him why. The tunnel itself gave me the creeps. I didn't want to know what else would make a god shudder.

In a straight line, we followed Hades, stepping where he did as we made our way further underground. The walls were a wet, slimy mess, the still-rotting corpses of other wanderers lumped in the corners. I tried not to heave, but the smell was horrendous, the air thick with decomposition. I was definitely getting *Temple of Doom* vibes from this place and that was not comforting at all.

Especially since my connection to the elements seemed... just *gone*.

Hades made one sure stride after the other, only stepping on the wide tiles that had an hourglass etched into them. A part of the floor possessed a deep crack, the fissure several feet wide. Hades attempted to jump it—which he succeeded—but he fudged the landing a bit. Hades stumbled onto another tile, and even though he tried to pull his foot back, the tile depressed with an ominous-sounding hiss.

I—along with the rest of the group—stood stock-still, waiting to see what kind of horror the maze would subject us to. I had a feeling it had something to do with water—at least based on the water-logged and rotting corpses, but what did I know? But no water came.

Instead, a smoky fog crept up from the fissure, coalescing into the shape of a woman. The woman stared at her transparent hands for a moment before turning to us. When she locked eyes on me, she partially solidified, and I nearly hit my knees.

"Maria?" I croaked, wanting to reach for her, but something held me back. Not something, someone. Alistair's arm was banded around my middle, holding me to him so I couldn't move. It reminded me so much of our trip to Hell. How he wouldn't let me fall into that great abyss.

I wanted to be comforted—that he wouldn't let me fall —but all I wanted was to reach for her. Why wasn't he letting me go?

Maria's face was a grayed-out ghost of what she once was, her expression sad and accusing all at the same time.

"You didn't follow me, sister. Why didn't you follow me?" she asked, her words hitting me like a slap. It was a question I'd been asking myself since she fell into that abyss. To have her voice it now when we were in this place, hit me harder than anything else she could have asked.

"I tried." My voice sounded like broken glass. "But I couldn't reach you before you fell. I tried," I pleaded, begging her to understand. "But you're here now. Come back to me, and we'll find Dušan. He said you were gone, but maybe he can get you your body back. He can help."

She smiled a sad little smile, a bitter pull of her lips that told me just how disappointed she was in me. "You were supposed to follow me. You were supposed to die, not me. I was meant to live, not you. Isn't that what you promised me? That I would live?"

I wanted to vomit. Of all the things Maria could say to me, I never thought she would want me to die. I tried to pull out of Alistair's arms, but his hold was iron-clad. Maybe if I could hug her, touch her, then she would realize that we could fix this. We could get her a body—if not the one she had, then maybe Dušan could make her another one. I could fix this...

"Please, just let me try to help. I can help."

Maria's face twisted, her lips snide, her eyes cruel. "You do nothing but cause pain and destruction. That is all you will ever be good for. Lachesis told me so. Sitting next to me in that frigid darkness she warned me of what you would bring." Maria tossed her head back, a mirthless laugh spilling from her lips. "All you bring is death."

Those last words were a hiss as her face decomposed right before my eyes. Her cheeks hollowed out, her skin shriveled to rot, her eyes yellowed before morphing into glowing embers, their light unearthly and cold. Maria took a shuffling step toward me, reaching for me, as if she wanted to drag me back down into that fissure with her and keep me there.

A sharp crack of a slap whipped across my cheek and I blinked. I shook my head, searching the room for Maria's corpse. Instead I found freezing waist-high water and my mother shaking the shit out of me.

"Wake the fuck up, Maxima." She yelled right in my face.

I blinked hard, shaking my head, slowly coming to the realization that Maria wasn't there. She wasn't... Loss hit me like a slap as my mother raised her hand again to knock some sense into me. Before her palm could connect with my already-sore cheek, I caught her wrist.

"I'm awake," I croaked, trying my best not to cry even though I knew it was likely inevitable.

Maria wasn't there. She was never there.

Alistair's hold on me turned from restraining to a kind of hug.

"Good. Now, remove the spell you cast to keep you entrenched in the corridor so we can pull you out." Teresa said it like she was talking to a half-crazed toddler on a sugar high.

Confused, I peered at my wrists. Glowing blue ropes were wrapped around them, their ends attached to the wet walls by nothing but magic as I hung between them. Sure. Yep, I could totally see myself doing some dumb shit like this. I pulled on the bonds, but they would not come undone. I mentally plucked at the spell, trying to rip the threads of it until I was free, but the water was rising and my mother and Alistair were still in here, and I had no idea how we were going to get out.

We didn't have enough time. There was never enough time.

Fear and shame hit me like a one-two punch, and I pulled again at my bonds. I yanked and wrenched, but they were immovable. Whatever magic I'd cast without realizing it was potent as hell because I couldn't break the spell.

"You guys have to go. Follow the others. Get out," I ordered. "I can't—I can't break the spell I cast."

Neither Teresa nor Alistair moved an inch, but it was Alistair who spoke. "Go, Teresa. I'll stay with her. Make sure the others get out."

He said it so calmly, so serenely. Like resigning himself to my fate was no big deal. Teresa blinked, her eyes turning lazy for a second before she nodded and half-slogged, half-swam away. Even in the low light, I could still see the threads of the working he'd cast with his voice. He'd spelled her so she would get out. I didn't know he could even do that.

And he'd done that for me.

I was still stuck on the wonder of it when he removed his banded arm around my middle and sloshed in front of me so he could look me in the eye. "Now, my love, I want you to call on whatever elements you have in your arsenal.

I want you to do whatever it is you have to do. But you and I are getting out of this bloody tunnel. There will be no dying. There will be no conceding. You are doing this, Max."

He wasn't going to leave. He needed to leave. I couldn't protect him. I couldn't protect anyone. Everyone got hurt because of me.

"No, love. I'm not leaving you. And no one gets hurt because of you. You can't control Fate and you can't take responsibility for everyone."

Until he said those words, I'd had no idea I voiced my concerns aloud. Unless he was reading my mind. That was always an option.

"Now think. What can you use to break a spell?"

Shivering at the aching cold seeping into my leathers, I tried to think. My athames could cut through spells. Maybe. Unless it had to be me that used them, and then we were likely fucked. "My athames?"

Alistair nodded, grabbing one blade from its sheath. In one swift motion, he sliced through the blue magical rope that held my right wrist and then moved to the left. Once I was free, the pair of us began the slog down the corridor, the water chest-high on us. But swimming in leathers and weapons was about as ineffective as carrying a bowling ball in a swimming pool.

Wanting to slap myself, I snapped my fingers, pressing

the water away from us, shoving it against the walls. Alistair and I fell to the tunnel floor, but he grabbed me up, setting me on my feet.

The power I needed to shove at the water was substantial, the use of it draining the shit out of me because there was just so much of it. No element could help me here, and it was too much water, too much power, too... I nearly fell, and rather than ask if I was okay, Alistair yanked me off my feet and tossed me over his shoulder, breaking into a run.

He was right to run, right to haul as much ass as he wanted.

Because I wasn't going to be able to hold this water for much longer.

CHAPTER NINETEEN

y poor, feeble spell began to break down almost immediately, the walls of water falling like dominoes as Alistair sprinted as if our lives depended on it. They kind of did, so I didn't fault the man. Instead I tried my level best not to pass out or let my magic fail. The trickle of my nose pouring blood was not at all comforting, though.

Again, we were running out of time.

Despite the water, the blue-flame torches flickered their eerie light, highlighting just how vast the tunnel was. And just how fucked we'd be if we didn't get out of here.

A commotion behind—or rather in front of Alistair— had a rush of relief hitting me even as I struggled to keep the water away from us.

"Run, man!" Barrett yelled, his voice frantic as it rang out over all the other voices.

Alistair picked up the pace, and then he pushed off the sodden ground and we flew the last hundred feet or so, his feet leaving the ground as he shoved off the tunnel floor with an enormous boost of power. Brightness bloomed across my vision right before we hit the ground. Somehow, Alistair not only knew how to fucking fly, but he'd also managed to turn us midair so he took the brunt of the fall and not me.

Still, his landing was not the best, the pair of us groaning at the impact before several hands yanked us away from the torrent of water rushing at us. I barely found my feet before I was unceremoniously plopped on the ground. My mother's hands patted me all over, searching for injuries, pressing healing talismans into my flesh wherever she could reach.

Damn, I must look really bad.

"Can't believe he did that to me. Damn demons and their bullshit mind control. I ought to skin him alive for that." My mother's tirade only got louder when I coughed and bloody black goo poured out of my mouth. "Taking me away from my daughter. If I knew it would hurt him, I'd set his demon ass on fire."

I wanted to tell her it looked way worse than it was,

but not only could I not articulate that particular state-ment, she wouldn't believe me even if I did. It was true, though. As soon as we were free of the tunnel, the elements made themselves known. Bit by bit, they filled me once again, their presence so welcome I would have sighed in relief if I weren't so busy yakking up bloody remnants of a spell gone bad. Alistair probably knew it would hurt me to sever the spell in that way, but he'd done it to save my life.

"Fucking backlash. Fucking demons. Just fuck this whole realm. Honestly. It's bad enough this maze is out of a bad imitation *Indiana Jones* movie, then I have to hear you scream Maria's name, too? I can only assume you saw her," Teresa hissed, not really asking me as she searched her bag for healing draughts and whatever else she thought she needed. "Stupid illusion magic."

I gasped an, "I'm fine," but she didn't even heed my words.

She kept searching for something in her bag. Letting out a blissful, "Ah, ha!" when she found what she was looking for.

"Don't make me shove my blood into you, Max," Della chimed in just as my mother unstopped a vial of glowing purple liquid of some kind.

All at once, she shoved it in my open mouth and then

did a thing that I'd seen Aurelia do with her son when he refused to take a nasty bit of medicine. As she shoved the vial in my mouth, she then tipped my head back and plugged my nose. The noxious liquid fell down my throat, and I had no choice but to swallow. I gagged, but there was nowhere to go and nothing to do. I couldn't spit it out, and I also couldn't shove my mother off of me.

As soon as the liquid was gone, she let me go so I could shudder at that particular injustice in peace.

"I was healing," I croaked, barely able to stifle a gag. "That was unnecessary."

Teresa rolled her eyes before leveling me with a "Mom look" so fierce it could have incinerated me on the spot. "You were not healing fast enough, and backlash can be fatal. Don't fuss at me, missy. It's bad enough I had to leave you in that damn tunnel. Don't push your luck."

"I'm not sorry, you know," Alistair groaned, flat on his back as he tried to catch his breath. "I couldn't have carried you both."

Teresa let out a growl which was only tempered by Andras wrapping her up in a hug. Andras whispered something in her ear and she sort of melted into him, letting out a shuddering breath as she buried her head into his chest. I'd scared her.

I looked around at the faces of my makeshift family.

Each one was a mask of fear and uncertainty. I met Barrett's gaze, his blue eyes shining with unshed tears as he rested his head on Marcus' shoulder. I'd scared them all.

"I'm sorry. I don't know what happened. One second Hades was jumping over the fissure and the next... it was Maria telling me I'd failed her and saying her death was my fault."

Hades let out a growl so fierce it was a wonder that my insides didn't shrivel on the spot. "It's one thing to do that to someone like me. It's quite another to make you think... I'll kill him. I'll fucking kill him."

I could only assume he meant Lucifer. I'd inferred this maze was concocted by Lucifer as a security measure for his castle. Or just a way to torture people. Really, it was dealer's choice at this point.

"What do you mean someone like you? You're no different than me."

Hades shook his head and stood, pacing a few steps away before he spoke. "I've been alive a very long time. When you've lived as long as I have, you do things you aren't proud of. Things you regret. The last time I sprung that trap, I saw something like what you did, a death I regretted but could not stop. I couldn't tell you how long I was in that tunnel, drowning over and over again, watching as the specter of my guilt bombarded me with shame."

Hades swallowed hard, like he was shoving his emotions down deep where they would never see the light of day.

"But that death was my fault. That blood will forever be on my hands. What happened to your sister was a cruel twist of Fate, and no matter how much guilt you feel, you are not responsible for her death."

I didn't like the way this conversation was going. I didn't want to hear one more person say I wasn't the reason Maria wasn't here anymore. Which was probably why I lashed out the way I did.

"And how in the fuck would you know? Were you in the Seam, watching us? Were you there when she fell?" I hissed, unable to stop myself from standing to confront him, getting right in his face like he wasn't an ancient deity. "Were you there when I didn't catch her? When I didn't protect her? When I waited too long to look for her? When I let myself get caught up in all the Ethereal drama and forgot that my first responsibility since the day she was born was to keep her safe? She's dead because Soren wanted to hurt me. She's dead because he saw her as nothing more than bait—as a way to trap me. So yes, I'm responsible for her death. Her blood is on my hands and will be until the day I die—whenever that will be.

There is nothing you can say that will make me think any different."

For some reason, I hoped that my tirade would have pissed him off. I wanted to fight something. I wanted to hit something—anything—as hard as I could. But Hades wasn't mad at me. Instead, his expression was awash in something like pity and it made me want to scream. It was tough, pulling myself out of the need to destroy, but I managed to refrain from hitting him and walked away.

I knew I shouldn't stray too far—the traps were likely everywhere—but I couldn't stay in that huddle being bombarded with everyone's grief and pity. The sky rumbled above us, the impending storm roiling with unspent raindrops. Soon, the clouds would burst, and lightning would slash the air overhead. I wondered if the rain would wash away this heaviness in my chest. If it would heal me like I wished it could.

Probably not.

I felt him coming long before I heard the steps, the finger-light touch of Alistair's power that I'd become accustomed to after such a short period of time. I was proved right a second later when his arms closed around me and he rested his chin on my shoulder. Having him at my back was a balm in a way I couldn't explain. Every time I was overwhelmed, every time I thought I couldn't press on one more step, Alistair was there to egg me on, push me just a little farther, make me push myself.

"Being possessed was no picnic, love," he began, his voice a gentle whisper in my ear. "But Hades saw everything I did in my memories. He saw us lose Maria. He saw what it did to you through my eyes. He knows all of it, love. Probably more than you want him to."

Great. Now I felt like more of an asshole than I already was.

"He—along with the rest of us—are allowed to be incensed at the atrocities done to you, love. We are allowed to mourn for the losses you've sustained. We are allowed to grieve with you. It is not pity or fear or shame. It is empathy, love. You don't have to go on like you were before—with only a few to care for you. You have a family now. You have people that love you. It's time to let go of the belief that you have to suffer this burden alone. Because you aren't anymore."

I wanted to be funny or deflect or something. I was ill-prepared for conversations such as these. Especially with someone I couldn't tell to fuck off. Turning in his arms, I gave him the unvarnished truth, staring into the beautiful blue eyes of his unphased form as I did so. "It's going to take some work to believe it," I admitted. "And then it will probably take a century's worth of reminders, so I don't forget. But I'm going to try. Okay?"

"That's all anyone can ask of you."

"Good. Now on to more important topics that have absolutely nothing to do with feelings or emotions or whatever," I quipped, waving my hand like I was wiping the slate clean. "You can fly?" Yes, it came out like an accusation, which was exactly as I'd intended.

Alistair blushed, his dimples popping as he gave me a shy smile. "I'm not very good at it yet. It'll probably take another fifty years or so to master the art of it. But we were in dire straits, and well, I figured it was better to try than not."

"So, you can *fly*." Again, the accusation was clear.

"I bet you could, too, if you tried hard enough. I'm sure the air element would likely help in that endeavor. I also assume with time you could breathe under water or move mountains. You can already do so much with so little time under your belt. Think of the possibilities."

For the first time, I stopped thinking of the time crunch we were under. About the maze or what would happen when we got Dušan back. Instead, I thought of our possibilities and what kind of future I wanted and who I wanted in it.

"That, love, is what I've been waiting for you to realize since you talked to me about fighting werewolves when we first met," he murmured against my lips, his breath mingling with my own as a sort of tentative peace washed over me. "The possibilities for you and I are endless. Just as we are endless."

It was a hope I didn't have before then.

A hope that would be dashed long before it could ever come true.

CHAPTER TWENTY

Before we really had a chance to rest, we were off again following Hades down a path that we hoped would lead us to Dušan. I felt no closer to the power that radiated across my skin, and even though the hope Alistair coaxed me to feel buoyed my spirit, I was sinking fast.

The sky swirled above us, the green-cast clouds churning with an impending storm that was not mine. I tried to think on the bright side. At least we weren't stuck in that stupid tunnel filled with rotten corpses or trying to bargain with a giant cyclops. Walking wasn't too bad—especially if I tuned out the ache in my feet and the nagging headache that had been building behind my eyes. The best I could do was draw on the elements to heal those aches and pains and press on, but the toll on my body and mind was wearing me down.

We slogged farther into the maze, following Hades as he picked his way through obstacles, stepping carefully in several places. Other than his misstep in the tunnel, we had yet to see another sprung trap.

We became complacent.

The time passing and aches in our bones and too many steps on too little sleep, made us forget that we were in enemy territory, playing a game built by the worst of the worst.

The path seemed clear, the sky above was ominous, sure, but it had been that way since we stepped foot into this section of the realm. There were no arches, no tunnels. Just a clear walkway unimpeded by anything. Which was why I was so stunned when Alistair shoved me from behind, knocking me to the ground. A slab of stone fell from nowhere, cleaving one part of our group from the other.

On my side was Lilith, Hades, and myself. On the other was Alistair, my mother and father, Barrett and Marcus, and Della and Hideyo. Somehow, I didn't think that was an accident.

"Alistair!" I yelled, hoping he could hear me through the slab. I only got that one yell out, though, because soon, my grandmother's hand was over my mouth, and she was dragging me away from the barrier. Darkness swept over my vision as she enveloped us both in a cloak of black smoke.

In the next instant, stone doors appeared in the walls where the rock had been solid moments before. Out of them poured dark elf soldiers, their weapons at the ready. Lilith's hold did not waver a single inch, and she dragged me with her as she attempted to put distance between us and the elves. I had no desire to be a conduit for her power ever again, so I didn't quibble, moving with her without so much as a peep.

I studied the elves. Their pale skin glistened in the low light. They looked so much like the ones in the cave, only less dirty, less unkempt, less feral. These elves had plaited hair, the braids smooth and unsullied by the filthy cave and decorated with silver wire and beads. While their features were just as sharp as their brethren, they moved with more purpose, as if they were on a mission from Lucifer himself.

"If you think we won't find you," an elf hissed, "you don't know your brother very well." His lips pulled back from his teeth as he spoke, showing shark-like incisors that made me glad I'd never gotten up close and personal with the cave dwellers. His warning was clearly meant for me, since Lucifer was my brother in the very loosest of senses. Somehow, they knew I was here. My only hope was that they didn't catch us before we found Dušan.

Yeah, I figured that was too much to ask the universe. I mean, why the fuck wouldn't it throw me a damn bone every once in a while, right?

"You can't hide from me, daughter of Chaos. We will find you," the dark elf called, and Lilith stopped moving, taking that moment to speak inside my head.

I can't stop them from finding us, Max. The best Hades and I can do is distract them while you run, but even that might not be enough. Dark elves are Lucifer's creation—they are imbued with his magic.

I wanted to tell her no, but I couldn't do it silently. I settled on shaking my head, willing her to understand that we should just stay put.

"Tick, tock, daughter of Chaos. If you don't show yourself, I will be forced to do something rather unpleasant. Maybe I'll find your fake mother and gut her in front of you. Would you like that? Or maybe your joke of a mentor. Barrett would make lovely noises when I strip his flesh from his bones."

That fucker was trying to get me to show myself, but I knew enough to know that if they planned on torturing the people I loved, they would do it whether I showed myself or not. I just had to pray my family didn't get caught.

"Very well, then." He sighed, seemingly resigned to doing things the hard way.

The magic in the air sizzled against my flesh as the elf pulled it into himself. His hands and eyes glowed an icy blue as he sucked the power from the air. Lilith's shroud flickered and then died, the darkness falling away from us.

Immediately, Lilith shoved me behind her, shielding me with her body as death magic erupted from her hands. The swirl of black magic hit the closest elf, withering his body to a husk where he stood. In less than a second, he was ash, crumbling to the ground. Lilith then let the magic spread outward, the noxious black tether jumping from elf to elf. It looked so different from the awful magic that erupted from me in the cave, but I could feel what it was—could see it.

Lilith knew the consequences of using this magic, but she was doing it anyway.

Hades jumped into the fray to help his sister, cutting down the elves closest to her that she hadn't yet touched with her magic. I would have, too, but Lilith suddenly had a hold on my wrist, her grip like iron as she pulled my power into herself. She fueled herself with it, draining me rather than pushing her power through me.

It ached. It burned. It felt like she would use me up, and I'd be no more than the husks of elves she'd already killed. I tried to yank my wrist away, but my weakness leveled me, knocking me to my knees as she took and took.

But just like her shroud of shadow, the head elf stole that power from Lilith, too, absorbing the dark magic into himself. He advanced, grabbing her by the throat. And as much as I wanted to, I couldn't stop him. All I could do was hit the dirt and pray that the elements didn't abandon me when I needed them the most.

There was only so much a girl could do against an army of dark elves—especially when said girl was unconscious. Cracking an eyelid, I groaned as a bolt of pain lanced my brain. Consciousness did not like me and was making that fact known. When I could blink both eyes open without wanting to either throw up or die, I studied the ceiling of what had to be a castle. Chandeliers filled with brilliant blue lights dotted the room. It wasn't until I could really focus that I realized the lights weren't flames at all.

They were caged sprites, their innate light flickering as they withered in their bonds. Just that alone made me want to throw up again, but I settled on letting my rage fuel me instead.

I could feel someone staring at me, the slimy caress of their attention sliding over my skin. Again, vomiting seemed like a good option, but I held my face expressionless. Something about the power signature in the room was both familiar and not, all at the same time. It wasn't the same as the bite of magic in the maze. No, that had to be Dušan. But this—unless I was way off base—was more than likely Lucifer, or Cronus, or whatever the hell he wanted to call himself these days.

As discreetly as I could, I pulled air into my lungs—a feat much different than merely breathing—drawing as much power as I could from the element. It came to me willingly, as did earth, trickling into me as I pressed my hand to the stone floor and shoved myself up to sitting.

Stalling, I cracked my neck, rolled my shoulders, and stretched my arms over my head, letting the elements heal me as much as they were able. Lilith had pulled too much from me, and I knew without a shadow of a doubt in my mind, I was at a severe disadvantage.

The room was cast in the eerie blue glow of dying sprites, and I studied it rather than let my gaze stray to the man whose eyes I could feel boring a hole in my cheek. High domed ceilings reminded me of the grand ballroom where I'd had my presentation to the Fates. Other than the fact that they were painted, that where the similarities ended. The scenes depicted on them were ones of torture and pain, eviscerations and beheadings.

The walls wept with moisture, the stone crumbling in some places from neglect, and the floor was filthy, strewn with leaves and detritus of inattention.

"Quit stalling, sister. Not looking at me won't delay the inevitable," a smooth British accent called, the power in it beckoning me to turn my head.

It seemed like ages ago when Micah Goode had transfixed me with his voice, and I wondered what would have happened if my glamour was gone like it was now. Because even with my power drained near to empty, I still gave Lucifer a mental *fuck you* and ignored him.

Rather than do what he said, I pondered if that was the reason so many did as he asked, why so many fell to his power. Was it his voice that lured them to do dark things, that convinced them to stray to the darkness in their own souls?

Or did people already have that darkness in them, and he just coaxed it to come out?

I supposed it was a question for the ages.

"Ah, so you are immune. No matter. My children are not. Would you like to see them attack each other? Or maybe you'd like to witness them gutting themselves?" He was so calm as he said this, like watching his children die was of no consequence.

As if he welcomed the idea.

Sighing, I tried to affect a bored expression. I met Lucifer's gaze, raising my eyebrows at him in the universal symbol of "what do you want?".

I didn't trust my voice at the moment because he was absolutely frightening in a way I could not name. It wasn't that Lucifer was ugly—he wasn't. In fact, he looked like a model. Chiseled features, blond hair, piercing blue eyes— nothing about him said grotesque. On Earth, he would be lauded for his beauty.

And it wasn't that he was huge—he was—but his size wasn't terribly foreboding. Close to six and a half feet, he wasn't even as large as Hades.

It had to be the air of utter confidence mixed with the crazed light in his eyes all combined with the blissful smile of a man at peace with the world—and his world was murder, torture, and death. It was the same quality I expected serial killers had when they'd found the perfect prey.

And his sights were set on me.

"That's better. I do so enjoy looking people in the eye when I torture them. It adds to the experience."

I snorted out a laugh that was so unladylike, and so totally me, it only made me laugh harder. What was he, a comic book villain? When my fit of giggles subsided, I couldn't help the zinger that fell from my lips. "What's next? Are you going to conjure a mustache just so you can twirl it? Honestly. Get better material."

Yes, I totally just laughed in Lucifer's face. The man who had kidnapped me, cut me off from my family, and was likely planning on killing me just as soon as he could.

Yep, no way that was going to backfire on me.

CHAPTER TWENTY-ONE

I didn't know exactly what I was expecting, but the gentle smile that bloomed across Lucifer's lips was not it. While I knew that smile was in no way a good thing, it was appreciated over an immediate smiting.

He sat forward on a black throne, the high-backed monstrosity playing at foreboding without hitting the mark. "Oh, I think my material is quite fresh. I mean, I've directly caused you to die one hundred and fifty times—give or take—without you even the wiser. I'm positive I'm doing just fine."

I blinked, stunned for a solid minute, but he kept talking, filling the gaps in my silence with his Machiavellian schemes. "First, I just wanted you out of the way. As Dušan's last-born child, you held claim to the Fae throne, and with it, the last true parcel of his power. I knew he wasn't true dead, but where he was, I couldn't follow. With you gone, I could claim your power as my own and snuff out Dušan once and for all." Lucifer tsked and shook his head, propping a booted foot on his knee, the picture of relaxation. "But you proved hard to kill. Like a weed, you just kept coming back. So, I decided to have a little fun. If I couldn't make you stay dead, I could make you miserable instead."

He sighed; his face wistful as another deranged smile bloomed on his face. "Humans are so easy to manipulate. I mean, burning you at the stake took practically nothing. And the stoning?" He chuckled at that one, shaking his head. "That was so simple, it was damn near criminal. And that hack of a doctor that dissected you while you were alive? Man, you took a long time to die. And on and on until Micah and Ruby and Samael and Elias and Soren. You know, all told, Verena was the hardest to convince to go along with my plan. She wanted more than the throne. She wanted the whole bloody realm. Silly girl. I do appreciate you killing her, by the way. Saved me from doing it."

All the times I'd died, it was Lucifer who was responsible. It was Lucifer as the puppet master the whole fucking time. I snorted before letting out the loudest fucking witch cackle I'd ever laughed. I was pretty sure his goal was for me to be pissed off and attack him or something, but all I could do was wipe my eyes as I just kept on laughing. I'd died *a lot*. And to find out none of it was my fault was a relief in a way.

"How annoying was it that I just kept coming back? I mean, at some point it kinda has to sting, right? I've been killed in *a lot* of ways, and no matter how many times you tried and no matter how many ways, I just kept giving you the middle finger and coming back to life. It is a relief, though. So, thanks for explaining it. I kinda just thought I was a little bit of an idiot. I kept getting myself into scrape after scrape, and lo and behold, it was you the whole time."

I dissolved into another fit of giggles, only this time, Lucifer was no longer a happy camper. No gentle little smile pulled at his lips, his genial nature long gone. "I tell you that I've killed you a hundred and fifty times, and you laugh? What's wrong with you?"

"What's wrong with me? More like, what's wrong with you? You're the chicken-shit bastard who can't gather the sack to kill me himself, and you wonder why I laugh in your face? You failed a hundred and fifty times to kill me. You failed in killing Dušan. You got locked up in a prison by your own children, and even when you escaped, I'll bet you couldn't worm your way out of this realm. Of course I'm laughing at you, Luci. You're utterly hilarious."

A booming guffaw practically shook the earth, the sound coming from behind me. I glanced over my shoulder to see Lilith and Hades tethered to the stone floor by glowing blue manacles. Hades was doubled over laughing, and I was sure he'd wipe the tears of mirth off his face if he could reach it. Lilith was trying to hold in her snickers but eventually gave up the ghost and began laughing with us.

I mean, what else was there to do? Lucifer had us, we were damn near out of time to get Dušan back to the tree, and all my family could be dead for all I knew. Why not laugh in the face of death himself? Why not knock him down a peg or two?

Because that was exactly what a man like that feared the most, wasn't it? People laughing at his worst?

"What else do you have for me, Luci? Are you going to kill me again? Ooh, or better yet, you'll torture me and make me watch as you rip out my liver. Or maybe you'll tie me to some train tracks or some other bullshit evil super-villain cliché. Again, my dear brother, you need better material."

Lucifer's rage ramped up so high I could feel it whipping against my skin. It swirled in the air around us without him so much as moving an inch. Out of the three of us, I was the only one untethered, but that was likely because I was the lowest threat. Lilith had syphoned off most of my power when she'd called her death magic forth. As much as the elements were feeding me, I wasn't at full strength yet.

"I have much more up my sleeve, sister, just you wait." With that he rose from his throne, his booted feet nearly shaking the ground as he descended a crumbling dais and made his way to his children. He stopped in between Lilith and Hades, his head waffling back and forth as he seemed to ponder something.

Lilith didn't wait for him to make a decision. She struck out with her booted foot, catching Lucifer right in the stomach before she yanked a no-longer-glowing manacle out of the stone floor. With the chain still attached to her wrist, she swung the links at her father's head, smiling with satisfaction when the chain wrapped around his throat. She yanked the other manacle out of the ground, lashing it at one of his wrists before she lifted herself up, planting her feet against Lucifer's chest.

Hades snapped his manacles, and instead of helping his sister, he ran at me, yanking me off the ground and taking off in a dead run. I tried to fight him—we couldn't leave Lilith alone with Lucifer—but Hades slapped me and roughly tossed me over his shoulder, never slowing his stride. Hades pumped his legs faster, but before we could even fully make it out of the room, we seemed to hit a brick wall, the force of the impact depositing the pair of us on the ground.

Lilith let out a frustrated screech, and instead of staying where I was, I ran back to her. Hades and Lilith had worked this out—trying to use her as a distraction to get me out—but it had failed, and I wasn't going to let her get killed if I could stop it.

I might not be at full strength, but I could help, dammit. The sizzle of electricity bloomed in the air as a bolt of lightning streaked across the room, hitting Lucifer right in the chest. He flew backward, sliding out of Lilith's hold as he hit the floor. I didn't make the same mistake as I'd made with Soren. Oh, hell no. I called down bolt after bolt, striking him over and over.

Lilith tried to get me to stop, tried to yank me away, but I wouldn't let her. Only when Lucifer began rousing, starting to stand up even though I kept hitting him, did I take in when Lilith had probably been screaming at me the whole damn time.

He is absorbing the power from the lightning. Stop hitting him!

My miscalculation was about to cost us, because no sooner did I stop hitting him, did he strike, volleying the electricity back at me. It would have been awesome if I could have absorbed it like he had, only I wasn't that lucky. The bolt slammed into me, making Lilith lose her grip on me as I flew back. I smashed onto the floor as the lightning arced over my body, sapping my meager strength and polluting me with Lucifer's special brand of poison.

Whatever he'd done to it after he'd drawn the electricity into him, he'd changed it somehow, making it so instead of helping me, it hurt.

I couldn't help it, I let out a scream of agony as bolt after bolt sizzled against my flesh. When the torture abruptly stopped, it took a second for me to get up. More like several seconds.

I managed to pull myself up to my hands and knees, my arms and legs shaking with strain. I nearly heaved when I struggled to standing, but I did it.

Lilith and Hades were trading blows with Lucifer, the siblings attacking in tandem. Lilith's death magic swirled around Lucifer as Hades' slashed at the ancient god with a glittering sickle. Black blood ran from Lucifer's cheek, as he fell to a knee.

And then it was like everything just stopped. The whole of the world stopped turning, the air stopped moving. Everything but Lucifer's hand as it whipped out, burying itself into Lilith's chest. Lilith froze, Hades skidded to a halt, but Lucifer kept right on moving, jerking his hand back, Lilith's heart now in his fist.

I couldn't say for sure if it was me that screamed or if it was Hades. Maybe it was the both of us. All I could see was Lilith's face. Her confusion. Her shock.

The color draining from her face as her body finally caught up to the fact that it no longer had an organ to keep the blood pumping. And then all at once the muscles in her face went slack as she fell, crumpling to the stone floor, her heart still in Lucifer's fist.

The ground quaked under our feet, the earth answering my scream of rage and pain as it split the floor in two. Hades pulled Lilith in his arms, dragging her from Lucifer, protecting her body with his own, even though she was gone.

She was dead. Lilith was dead. It's my fault. I taunted him, I filled him with power, I did this.

Hot tears hit my cheeks as I screamed, letting the earth pitch and quake. I hoped it would take this whole realm down. I hoped it would split this whole place in two, crumble it to ash and dust.

My rage only intensified when Lucifer started laughing. "You think a little earthquake is going to stop me? I've been alive since the dawn of time, and I'll be here after you taste clay, little girl."

That might be so, but dammit, if I was going down, he was coming down with me.

I didn't care if I had to bring this whole fucking realm down when I did it, either.

CHAPTER TWENTY-TWO

ALISTAIR

There were many things I would do for my wife. I would go to war for her. I would battle with her at my side. I would swallow my worry and fear and keep my promise to never stand in her way. But I swore to myself if she didn't make it out of this bloody maze, if she was lost to me, I would scour the dregs of this realm and every other until I found her again.

I didn't care what favor I'd have to call in, what deal I'd have to make. I was getting her back. *I was.*

Why did you push her? You should have grabbed her, pulled her back. Why did you do that?

My self-flagellation had been running on a solid loop for the last little bit, ever since that stone slab cut me off from my Max. *My Max.* She was mine, and Lucifer himself wasn't taking her from me. Not if I had anything to say about it.

Max and I had never discussed what happened to a demon when they mated. The bone-deep need to protect, to possess, to make a home in their soul and never let go. So few demons mated, the process arcane and little used anymore. There was no such thing as divorce. No such thing as irreconcilable differences—not that didn't result in death, anyway.

I supposed it didn't matter since Max was likely a goddess and not the demon princess we'd thought she was. The signs had been there, sure. Her perceptions of magic, how it smelled, how she saw the threads of it. The way she could bend the elements to her will, even under a glamour so powerful it locked most of her abilities away.

As soon as Andras removed it, I'd figured she was a Fae—I mean the ears were a dead giveaway—but her power signature was so much more than what she appeared. I wasn't the only one. The whole of Hell knew it, too. The ground rose up to meet her, the animals treated her as if she was their queen. The souls wished to touch her, share her light.

And then by an odd twist of Fate, she became my wife. I didn't know how I'd gotten so lucky—to have her love me, accept me. Even with the blight of my family, of my father.

Somehow, she didn't even blame me for Maria. Even though it was my father who dragged her down with him. Even though his blood still flowed through my veins.

A shove abruptly knocked me into the maze wall as a minotaur nearly gored me to death, the pungent scent hitting me harder than the wall. Della wiped blood from her nose before reaching out to help me up.

"Get your head in the game, Knight," she hissed and readied her sword, preparing to get the damn thing once and for all.

So far, we'd come across a hydra, a minotaur, three flooded passages, a fissure in the ground that probably went all the way to the heart of the realm, and a fucking Arachne. All of us were either hurt, tired, or just plain pissed off. Mostly all three.

The minotaur scraped back a booted foot, readying himself to charge when I heard the telltale snap of a witch casting a spell. Barrett's hands were coated in the reddish purple of his magic before the spell flowed to fruition. Not a second later, the minotaur's head exploded like a watermelon at a Gallagher show, blood and gore hitting the maze walls and floor in a gut-churning splat.

"You could have done that the whole bloody time, you bastard," Andras griped, wiping mushy organ remnants off his face and flicking them off his fingers in disgust. "Way to go exploding his head right when I'm next to him."

I kind of wanted to laugh. I knew without a shadow of a doubt in my mind Max would have been laughing if she'd seen it. But that fleeting thought brought back the fact that she was out there somewhere, maybe hurt, maybe dying, and I could not get to her. I thought about all the times Max had been in trouble. All the times when I felt it down deep in my bones that she needed my help.

Absentmindedly, I rubbed my thumb over the obsidian pendant she'd given me right after our first kiss. It was how I found her that night in the clearing. It was how I found her in New Orleans. It was how I knew where she was after Striker had taken her. I wanted it to work right now. I wanted it to tell me where she was so I could go get her. Why wasn't it bloody working?

"Alistair?" Marcus called, and I shook myself out of my musings to glance at him. Like me—like all of us—he was several steps past worry. Max had a family now, and all of us cared for her. All of us were frightened that we wouldn't see her again.

"Yes?" I replied, my throat clogged with all the fear and rage and worry I'd tried so hard to shove down deep.

"She gave you that pendant, yeah? Maybe—"

"Do you think I haven't already tried?" I hissed. "All I can feel is that burning power against my skin. All I can see in my head is this bloody maze. I don't know if it's Dušan or her or if she's... if she's..." I couldn't finish that sentence. Not out loud. Not where the universe in all its cruel twists of Fate could hear me. If I said it aloud, the Fates might make it so. They might take her from me.

Teresa approached, threading an arm around my waist and giving me a squeeze. It was a wholly mom gesture, one I'd never felt from my own mother. Isolde Quinn had never been the mothering kind. Neither had Teresa if history told the tale, but she was trying.

"We will find her. I know in my soul we will. We will find her healthy and whole and she will outlive us all. Now, instead of thinking the worst, tell me what you see when you hold the obsidian. If it doesn't lead to her, it could lead to Dušan. Maybe if we find him, we can find her."

Teresa was talking sense, but I had no illusions that this would work. We'd likely find more of the same—more monsters, more obstacles, more risk to our lives because Lucifer was a petty cunt with nothing but time on his hands. She could see the apprehension on my face, because I got a scolding only a mother could provide.

"Stop stalling and do it, Alistair. Whomever we find is a step in the right direction—is a step toward my daughter."

I gave her a sharp nod, shoving my trepidation down deep where it couldn't spill out of my mouth. Closing my fist around the obsidian amulet, I shut my eyes and waited for that pulling sensation I'd felt each time I needed to find Max. My feet moved me, knowing the direction even when I didn't. In my mind's eye, all I saw was the craggy stone maze walls and the detritus of bones of the other travelers scattered about. Without my telling them to, my feet picked up the pace, hopping from one side of the corridor to the other, dodging obstacles as I ran.

The zing of power raking across my skin got sharper, the feeling so much like Max but wholly different. I knew this wasn't her deep down in my bones, and I hoped her magic wasn't leading us into a trap. I opened my eyes as I rounded the final corner, braced for whatever we would find.

Max's athame practically vibrated in my hand, the power in it calling to someone or something else. I hadn't had the chance to give it back to her after the tunnel, and even though it hurt to hold onto it, I knew I couldn't let it go. And as soon as we turned the corner, I saw exactly what had been calling to me, calling to the blade.

A giant of a man stood stretched between the maze walls, his arms pulled wide by glowing blue ropes. I'd seen those ropes before. They were the same damn magic that held Max in the tunnel and damn near let her drown. The man—whom I could only assume was Dušan—was easily seven and a half feet tall. His short dark-purple hair waved in a nimbus cloud above his head as if he were underwater. Glowing gold eyes reminded me of his daughter's, his wide mouth too much like hers as well.

Before him was a grayed-out woman holding a baby, the faint blue cast to her hair a less vibrant version of the swaddled daughter in her arms. The woman was being stabbed in the chest over and over by an unseen hand, the shock and betrayal on her face warring only with the pain. She screamed, pleading for the unseen person to stop, to not take her away from her daughter, but the scene continued to play out, never changing as it stopped, reset, and played again.

All the while, Dušan begged his wife to run, to not trust her sister, to take their daughter away from Faerie. He screamed as he struggled against the bonds, but they did not waver, and he could not get out.

I met Teresa's gaze and gave her a sharp nod. Teresa had done what I could not in the tunnel: slapping Max to snap her out of the illusion. Teresa appeared wholly unprepared to slap the shit out of the father of the gods, though. She visibly swallowed before she sprang into action, sprinting through the illusion and leaping up to knock the ever-loving shit out of Dušan. Teresa didn't give him a piddly little slap. Oh, no. She cocked her fist back and slammed her knuckles into his jaw, whipping his head back hard enough to give the man whiplash. Deity or no, that punch looked painful.

Dušan sputtered, shaking his head and blinking furiously.

He locked eyes with Teresa, her tiny body dwarfed by his. His expression wasn't angry, though. No, Dušan seemed relieved, his shoulder sagging as much as the magical ropes would allow.

"Thank you, kind witch," he rumbled, his voice exactly what I would have thought the father of gods voice would sound like. "You are my Massima's mother, yes?"

Teresa took a step back, her chin jutting high before she nodded.

Dušan's gaze swept over us all. "You all are her family." He nodded as if he was coming to grips with something before he yanked on his bonds. The blue ropes stretched but did not break. "My son's power is formidable," he murmured to himself before gritting his teeth and yanking again. The ropes refused to let him go.

"Max was under a similar spell. I can get you out," I offered, pausing before tacking on a condition. "But only if you are here to help. Only if you're going to stop Lucifer from killing Max, unless you are going to act against him. Lucifer does not deserve your mercy, and if you're just going to let him get away with all that he has done, then I won't help you."

Dušan appraised me for a few long moments, his unsettling gold gaze leveling me where I stood. "Lucifer will die today, my son. He will pay for his crimes. I swear on the soul of my beloved, on the souls of my lost children, on the very fabric of this realm, and all the others I helped create. He. Will. Pay."

I must have hesitated a touch too long because Barrett snatched Max's athame out of my grip, striding over to the giant god with a purpose. "Well, that's good enough for me, Dušan. How about we get those bonds off you? Be warned, your daughter experienced an unhealthy dose of backlash from this, so… gird your loins."

Barrett cleaved through the blue magic, and the earth was still for one blissful moment before it pitched, knocking us all to our feet. A shockwave of power blasted from the cut bond, knocking Barrett away as spent power exploded through the corridor. Dušan bent, snatching up the athame, the blade dwarfed in his big hand. Without warning, he slashed through the other bond, a twin blast ricocheting off the walls as it settled over us all. Dušan fell to his knees, sucking in huge breaths.

And then we heard it.

Somewhere—even though she had to be miles away— all of us heard Max screaming.

CHAPTER TWENTY-THREE

Tiny dribbles of blood fell from Lucifer's fingers, the minuscule drops inaudible as they hit the stone. But I felt each one. Each drip scored wounds into my soul in a way I knew I'd never heal.

The ground pitched violently under my feet, the whole of the realm reaching up to those drops of blood. Wind whipped through the chamber, carrying debris on the gale as it thrashed around us. Lightning stabbed the ground around me, the fire and electricity reaching for me. Clouds roiled against the domed ceiling, the water in them begging to be set free.

Maybe the elements thought I needed their comfort. Perhaps they waited for me to send them to do my bidding. Or maybe they were just as mad as I was and wanted their revenge.

Lucifer didn't spare me a glance even though I was the biggest threat in the room. Instead, he dropped Lilith's heart, his careless fingers flinging her blood on the stone floor as he studied his son. Hades was still clinging to Lilith, her slack limbs akimbo as he dragged her lifeless body back with him, refusing to leave her to their father.

Lucifer advanced on his son, but not for long. The floor opened up between them, cracking the earth so deep it reached the heart of the realm. Flames rose from the earth, forming a wall separating father and son, answering my call. The fire changed shape, the flames morphing into the head of a dragon snapping at a startled Lucifer. He fell to his ass on the stone as the fire coiled around Hades, protecting him as I should have protected his sister.

Lucifer whipped his head to me, focusing on me like he should have before. He might want to spite his children, but I was the threat in the room. I was his undoing. I was his punishment.

"So you want my attention, sister? Well, now you have it. So eager to die?"

Now was not the time for pithy dialogue and witty banter. There was nothing to say, no reasoning that would change his mind. No stalling. It was him and me, and we were at the end of a very long road.

"You know whatever you do to me, I will just steal your power for my own. I'll twist it against you." His voice was a sing-song taunt, reminding me how I'd gotten Lilith killed in the first fucking place. He didn't need to recap my failure. I'd remember until I stopped breathing.

No, I had no plans to hit Lucifer directly. My intentions were to hit around him, encasing him in a living prison until one of us died, or I figured out a way to seal him away forever.

Because he wasn't doing this to anyone else. He wasn't taking any more lives. He wasn't going to poison another soul. Not if I could help it.

Lightning streaked across the room, the bolt hitting the stone just at his feet instead of striking him directly. Each bolt was one spoke in a wheel-like cage, drilling into the ground, burrowing deeper into the earth. The burgeoning clouds began to burst, their water falling in a torrent before each drop moved to reinforce the cage. Fire was next, the flame dragon swirling around Lucifer's makeshift cell in a maelstrom of heat.

Lucifer began to scream obscenities at me, but I couldn't hear them over the howling wind that added itself to the barrier, carrying bits of earth with it. Each layer whirled in a widdershins circle, each one undoing, unmaking. Each layer a *break* all on their own, denying him power. He wanted to try to use my elements against me? He wanted to sully them, spoil them? I didn't think so.

I pushed the elements as hard as I could, giving everything to the cage, taking nothing for myself. I couldn't let him out—not after what he'd done, not after what he intended to do. But I'd already been drained by Lilith, already had spent too much of myself.

The telltale trickle of my nose bleeding gave me my first niggle of doubt. I didn't have enough power to hold him. I'd gotten cocky, already planning Lucifer's checkmate before reality set in. Lucifer was older than time, older than this realm or any of the others, and I thought a *break* was going to hold him?

Lucifer's lips curled in a triumphant smile as he studied my face, his grin stretching wide when he caught sight of the blood on my skin. He knew—just like I did—that I wouldn't be able to keep him caged.

That I would fail.

Slowly, he found his feet, fighting my *break* far easier than I would have thought he could. Lucifer began pushing against the walls of his makeshift cell, not even flinching as the power of the spell abraded his skin. It brought me to my knees when—even though he shouldn't be able to—he began drawing the elements into him.

I wanted to rip them away, steal them back from him, but I couldn't. Even in that cage, Lucifer cut through my elements like a hot knife through butter, liberating himself and stealing from me all in one fell swoop. The shockwave of the cage crumbling swept through the chamber, lifting me off my knees and slamming me against a far wall. I landed flat on my back, air refusing to go back into my lungs.

Lucifer took his time coming for me, letting me claw at my own throat as I struggled to breathe. Oh, but when he did? He gave me back my elements ten-fold, each one poisoned.

Each one wrong, tainted.

The fire raked across my skin—not the loving caress that healed, but a blistering flame that would have wrenched a scream from me had I been able to make one. My skin burned away, my hair. The spells in my leathers no match for Lucifer's brand of poison. Bits of earth pelted my ruined flesh, the wind carrying them like tiny knives that embedded into my skin. And then the water came. It was like acid, burning away any flesh that the fire had left behind.

I could feel the elements try to reach me, try to heal me, but they were no match for Lucifer. The man in question practically giggled as he watched me choke and writhe, my body refusing to let him win, even if my brain had finally caught on that I wasn't ever going to. My legs pushed my body back, my hands scrabbled, looking for purchase on the stone floor so I could get away.

But I knew.

I would die just like Lilith had, like Hades would as soon as Lucifer remembered he had a son.

Lucifer knelt at my side, his still-bloodstained hand reaching for my heart. All I saw was a streak of gold and black as someone tackled Lucifer, knocking him away from me.

"You will not harm her," Hades screamed at his father, his form fading back and forth between the gold visage of Hades and his former smoke-monster shape. He stood tall, blocking Lucifer from killing me. "You might be able to steal from her, but you and I both know you can't steal from me, old man."

Lucifer tossed his head back and laughed, and Hades didn't waste that opportunity. He morphed into smoke and flew at his father's chest, knocking Lucifer farther back. When he recovered, Luci's smile was long gone.

"If I have to go through you to get to her, I will. Just like your sister, you chose the wrong side. You would think after centuries as you are, you would have learned that there is nowhere you can go, nothing you can do to deliver yourself from me. I will *always* win. I am inescapable."

The earth suddenly pitched, nearly knocking both Hades and Lucifer to the ground.

"As am I," a voice boomed. A voice I knew. A voice that was as welcome as the scant air in my lungs.

With my last bit of strength, I managed to turn my head to the voice, the weight of pain nearly crushing me, but I did it. A giant of a man stood there along with some very welcome faces. Dušan. My family.

I would have breathed a sigh of relief if I could have. Alistair broke ranks, coming to me and ignoring everyone else.

"Fates, Maxima. *Fates.*" His voice was clogged with tears, and I couldn't figure out why. I was so happy to see him, so happy. "Someone help me," he screamed. His hands fluttered over my body, as if he couldn't figure out where to touch me that wouldn't hurt.

Barrett and my mother's heads entered my field of vision, their forms swimming since I was crying tears of relief. Lucifer wasn't going to win. They had found Dušan and he would fix this. He would stop his son. I likely wasn't going to be around to see it, but I could feel the weight of expectation lift from my shoulders.

Struggling to swallow, I wanted to tell them how much I'd miss them. How much I loved them.

"Don't you leave me, Max. You hold on. We can fix this," Alistair ordered, his voice a fierce whisper as he laid on his belly right next to me, his face now on my level. He wouldn't touch me, but I could feel him anyway, and his presence was a relief even if the agony of my wounds were stealing the life from me.

He would live. They would all live.

And then with a single booming snap, the pain went away. My body started healing itself, Lucifer's poison leaving me instantly. It should have hurt—the re-growing of my flesh and hair, the healing of my muscles and organs —but it didn't. I sucked in one glorious breath after the other, my tears of relief falling in earnest. My body lifted on its own, Dušan's power giving me back everything Lucifer had taken.

I watched as my skin knitted back together, my tattoos blooming once the flesh was healed. I was naked for a single moment before a scarlet dress covered my body.

Alistair scrambled to standing, reaching for me. His fingers closed over mine and he pulled me to him, wrapping me up in his arms as his lips fell on mine. Our kiss broke almost instantly as the room's vibe hit us.

"You dare try to take another child from me?" Dušan growled, his power whipping through the chamber. "Of all the atrocities you've done, and you try this, too?"

Lucifer took a step back, his gaze searching the room for exits.

My gaze fell on Andras. He, too, had broken ranks and was cradling his mother's lifeless body in his arms. Lilith's dark hair fell in a waterfall over his arm as he buried his face in her neck. As happy as I was that I was alive, that we could win, that I wasn't alone anymore, my heart broke all over again.

"What was it you said to your son?" Dušan boomed, "'There is nowhere you can go, nothing you can do to deliver yourself from me.' I know it was you, my son. I know you did all of this. I know what your plans are. And no, you will not succeed."

Hades and Dušan moved in tandem, launching their huge bodies at Lucifer. Hades' smoke form wrapped around Lucifer's like a vine, binding the man so he couldn't move.

"Massima?" Dušan called. "I require your assistance."

Confused as to what I could do that they could not, I slowly picked my way to them, careful of the bits of sharp stone until I was smart enough to conjure myself a pair of combat boots. Say what you want about fashion, but a Grecian-style dress and combat boots totally went together.

Apprehension twisted in my gut, but I stood tall as I approached, my Knight just behind me. The heat of him seeped into my skin, warm and comforting and steady.

"You, alone, can stop him in a way I cannot. You, alone, can end his reign of terror." At my baffled expression, he continued, "Unlike any other god, you can alter Fate, bending it to your will. You have done it many times already. To Finn and Elias and Verena. You can change the threads of Fate, turning the long-lived mortal again."

Realization dawned. "Did you do this on purpose?"

Dušan shook his head. "I am master of many things, but I cannot alter Fate. Only you can. I ask that you use that power now."

With pleasure, I thought, not knowing if Dušan could hear me but hoping he could. Just like with Finn that first time, I pressed my three center fingers into Lucifer's sternum, my thumb and pinky spread wide.

"This is for my sister. My mother. For Lilith. This is for every life you've taken, everyone you imprisoned. I hope you fucking choke on it."

And just as I did with the wayward werewolf, I turned my hand to the right like a key in a lock, cutting Lucifer off from every ability, every power. The putrid motes swirling around his head like a macabre crown, the ones that told of his god-like power, fizzled and died.

We enjoyed the bliss of our win for one fleeting second.

And then the world began to fall apart.

CHAPTER TWENTY-FOUR

L ucifer's laugh could be heard over everything. Over the walls of the dark castle crumbling, over the ceiling cracking and falling in. Over the whole of the Unseelie realm falling apart.

Even mortal, Lucifer was a crafty fucker, and he'd already thought of the one thing that could checkmate us all. He'd created the Unseelie realm, and with his magic turned off, this whole fucking place would crumble to nothing.

That laugh grated, and I had the good sense to take his voice away with a snap of my fingers.

There. That was better.

"Time to get the fuck out of here," Alistair muttered, grabbing my hand and yanking us body and soul out of the castle.

I'd known he could transport himself, but like Aidan, I'd assumed his traveling would make me vomit. It was nothing like that—or maybe after Dušan healed me, I was different now. It wasn't like when I transported myself. It wasn't a blink-and-you-miss-it kind of thing. Instead, an ephemeral black smoke propelled us through space and time, unmaking and remaking us in an instant.

Alistair landed at the entrance to the maze where we'd left Aidan and Zillah. Their protections gone, as Aidan faced off against Argus. Argus' bonds had to have fallen off when I'd cut off Lucifer's magic, and he hadn't hesitated a minute in finding mischief. Aidan's sword was drawn as he protected the seemingly young Zillah against the cyclops.

"You dirty fucking rat," I yelled, getting both their attentions. Argus spared me a glance, but it was the relief on Aidan's face that made me mad as hell.

Others in our party landed seconds after we did, but it wasn't until Dušan stood tall next to me, a struggling Lucifer in his grip, did Argus stop advancing on Aidan. Oh, so now that Daddy was here, he was acting right.

Well, fuck that.

But before I could hand Argus his ass, the world pitched and swayed, the cacophony of the castle and maze crumbling in earnest stole my attention.

"Leave, son of Gaia," Dušan rumbled, his voice louder

than the realm falling apart. "Do not make me tell your mother what you have done to those under her protection. This realm is not for you. I suggest you find other accommodations before your choice is taken from you."

Argus' face paled, and without so much as a word, he gave Dušan a truncated bow before loping off into the trees.

Without mercy, I stalked over to Aidan and thumped him right on the head. "You were supposed to get out of here, stupid. Facing off against a fucking cyclops. Gah! It's amazing you made it this long."

Aidan rubbed his temple, staring down at me like a big brother would when taken to task by his little sister. "You weren't back yet."

Frustrated, I let out a growl but still touched his forehead with a single finger, fully healing his idiotic ass. Then, I did the same to Zillah, only he still refused to wake up. "Pick him up and find a buddy. It's time to blow this popsicle stand."

"Daughter?" Dušan called, snagging my attention. "I will carry us to the bridge. Do not try to travel across it by magic. The river keeper is not one you should cross."

I rolled my eyes. *Now he tells me.* "Pip is a friend and should be expecting us."

Dušan's smile was knowing, and I had a feeling he was reading my mind right now as I thought about what happened the last freaking time I tried to cross that damn bridge. I only got to enjoy that smile for a moment before all of us were pushed through space and time, landing at the edge of the bridge.

Pip appeared surprised to see us, especially the magically neutered Lucifer. Their fishy eyes went wide as they studied the lot of us. The bridge was not the one I wanted to cross, the vines rickety and rotted. Nope. Even though I knew I wasn't going to die, I needed a solid surface to walk on.

"No time to waste, Pip. The bridge, please."

Pip blinked in shock, but snapped their fingers, the vined bridge morphing to stone. The majority of us crossed, but Pip stood tall in front of Andras, his arms curled around Lilith's body as he tried to bring her with him.

"The dead cannot cross here," Pip commanded, their staff hitting the ground at Andras' feet.

Andras' whole body shook as he yelled at the river keeper. "This whole bloody place is falling apart, you damned fish. I am not leaving her here."

Fates, his pain was my own. I wanted to sob, but it was Pip's next words that shook me.

Pip's eyes turned sad but repeated themselves, sadness laced in their tone. "The dead cannot cross the river, son of Lilith. Kiss her goodbye and leave this place. She would want that for you. It is what I would want for my child."

Andras looked like his soul was being ripped in two, but he placed a kiss on his mother's forehead, laying her at Pip's feet.

"I will watch out for her, son of Lilith. She will be safe with me." Pip reached to hold Lilith's limp hand, sitting in the center of the bridge, ready to settle in for the end.

"Pip? You need to cross. This realm isn't going to make it." That should be obvious. The ground was trying its level best to fling us into space.

Pip looked over their shoulder, their large, sad gaze meeting mine. "The dead cannot cross here, daughter of Chaos. Those without a soul cannot traverse Styx. It is forbidden."

Two things became clear. One, the river Styx flowed through Faerie, specifically the Unseelie realm. And two, Pip was dead and soulless. And trapped in a crumbling realm. Tears hit my eyes for them.

"It's time for you to leave this place, daughter of Chaos. Do not fear. I will be at rest soon enough."

And then we were swept away, Dušan carrying us through the forest of sentient trees to the gate. Naturally, the gate was blocked by a host of pissed-off trees and a phased dragon ready to breathe fire.

It was Striker who saw us first, a relieved expression on his dragon face.

A sharp whistle assaulted our ears a split second later, and Marcus—who looked like he was fed the fuck up—marched toward the horde. His words were garbled as he let loose his tirade, likely because he had too many teeth in his mouth, the phase changing his features even though it shouldn't.

"Listen up," he commanded. "Unless you want to die, I suggest you knock it off and let us pass. This realm is collapsing, and you are very dangerously treading on your word."

The trees parted, and rather than have their deaths on my soul, I figured amnesty was a better course of action. "It isn't safe here. If you are deemed worthy by Dušan, you may enter the Seelie realm and set down roots. If you would rather stay, I won't stop you. Make your decision quickly, though. This place won't last much longer."

I glanced over to Dušan, a proud smile on his face at my pronouncement. He nodded slightly, and I had a feeling most, if not all of the trees would be making a new home in Faerie proper.

The giant sentient trees moved to let us pass, and we approached the gate. Striker, proving he was a man of his word, stayed put, guarding the portal like he swore he would.

"Yo, man. You aren't gonna fit. Time to phase back," I called to him.

I watched in amazement as his form shrank, his limbs and body forming his human shape once again. Unable to help it, I gave my friend a hug, grateful he was still here.

As our party approached the cliff face where the portal had once been, my apprehension about how we would get back to the Seelie Court ramped up. Aiyana had said she could not see this side of the gate. If she couldn't see this side, how was she to know we were here? And if she couldn't see, would the gate even open for us?

Dušan swept past us holding a still-struggling Lucifer in one hand and laying his other against the rock. I felt a pulse of power in the air, and I hoped Aiyana could hear his beacon. All at once, the stone cracked, the cliff face splitting. I had a sudden worry that Lucifer's removed powers were affecting this, too, when light poured out of the crack. The gate was opening, and it was larger than the one we'd had before. Stretched a few hundred feet tall and just as wide, it seemed tailored specifically for the beings walking through it.

Huh. I guessed that whole "no magic" credo for the gate only applied to beings that weren't Dušan. I was sort of fine with that.

He turned to the trees, speaking in that guttural language I did not understand. I sort of hoped he was telling them all to come with us, but I had no way of knowing for sure. Well, until Hades leaned over to whisper in my ear.

"He's letting them come to the Seelie realm. Well, his actual words were, 'There is no way I'm telling a creation of Gaia that they must die so we can live. If she disagrees, she can kill you herself, but it won't be me doing it.' Which is smart. Gaia really hates it when her creations are destroyed."

Good to know. I didn't understand exactly, but we were so close to the end, I did not give that first fuck. We traversed the gate, me holding Alistair's and my mother's hand, and we stepped into the Seelie realm for the first time in what seemed like eons. We couldn't have been gone more than a day, but it felt like we'd been gone years.

The crevasse was dark, the sun gone and a full red moon above us.

The Blood Moon.

CHAPTER TWENTY-FIVE

Dušan wasted no time with ceremony or pleasantries. There was no discussion or lighting of candles or whatever. No. The Blood Moon was overhead, and we had officially run out of time. With Lucifer in tow, he strode to the ancient tree that had almost brought his demise. Dušan laid a giant hand on the bark in an almost gentle caress, coaxing Aiyana to answer him.

But confusion hit me hard when he began to speak.

"Gaia, mother of worlds, I seek your audience."

Gaia? But I thought... She introduced herself as Aiyana. Then I snorted. It totally made sense once I remembered that half of the people I'd met had two names. Hell, even I had two names. Dušan was Chaos, Bernadette was Lilith, Niall was Hades, Lucifer was

Cronus, and I was Massima. The pain that still throbbed in my heart lanced sharper when I thought of Lilith.

We would never be able to bury her. Never be able to put her to rest.

My thoughts were stolen when a fissure of light cracked in the tree's trunk. The light grew wider, as a delicate bare foot stepped out of the bark followed by the rest of the goddess I'd once thought of as Aiyana. Clad in a midnight-blue floaty dress, emerged from the tree in a way only a goddess could.

Okay, only in a way that a goddess who was not me could.

Her silvery-white hair flowed down her shoulders, the strands decorated with cuffs and braids and intricate loops. Her horns glowed blue in the low light along with the crescent moon on her forehead, her shining arctic eyes searching the crowd. Only after she met the eyes of each of us did she finally land on Dušan and the struggling Lucifer.

Even at the end, Lucifer was hell-bent on not being in Dušan's arms.

"The Blood Moon is nigh, Chaos. What have you brought me to pay your debt?" she announced, and it took a second for me to understand.

The bargain was with her. *She couldn't say,* my fabulous ass. She didn't *want* to say when I'd asked her who the

QUEEN OF FATE & FIRE • 239

bargain was with. But what they had bargained for didn't make sense for what—*and why*—they would have made one in the first place.

Dušan rose to his full height, staring Gaia down with an expression so formidable I wanted to take a step back. "This bargain was struck because you refused to end our son's life. In exchange for his imprisonment, you bade me to give you a sacrifice every five hundred years. Cronus is no longer imprisoned, so I will sacrifice no longer."

Gaia appraised her son, her face not the kind mask she'd worn before, but the bitter judgment of a disappointed mother. I knew that face all too well from my youth.

"You had to have known our son had broken free long before my family was killed, my former wife. For that you will owe me until the end of days. Your omission cost the lives of thousands. Your deception nearly unmade everything we created. Nearly took everything from us."

Oh, Dad was *pissed*. I was, too. Gaia's omission killed my birth mother, my sister, Lilith, and how many others? How many times had someone lost their lives because of Lucifer?

"Our union ended before time began. All I have of it are my children," she murmured, and I about lost my fucking mind.

Somehow, Alistair knew I was about to lose it because

he wrapped his arms around me from behind, his gentle, calming touch ramping down my rage to a burning simmer of hatred.

All she had was her children? And what about all the other children Lucifer had taken? What about the ones he locked away or forced into servitude or straight-up murdered or…

"And how many of our children and grandchildren has Cronus injured? How many has he tortured or raped or played with like toys for his own amusement? Your refusal to see what he is, isn't going to change him. Caging him did not change him. He must be no more, Gaia."

Gaia shook her head in denial, her gaze landing on her son once more. She finally seemed to realize that he wasn't like he'd used to be as he struggled with human strength against his father.

"What have you done to him?" she asked, affronted.

She had the actual nerve to be *affronted*? I had to focus on Alistair's arms around me so I didn't pop off on the mother of creation, but the threat of me doing that was so real, it actually hurt my insides not to.

"Not me, former wife. My daughter did what you could not. She took away Cronus' power, took away his immortality. He will live and die as a man—as he should have eons ago when we discovered his vile nature."

Gaia's gaze moved from Dušan to me, and I couldn't

help myself, I gave her a finger wave and a shitty grin. If I couldn't tell her to fuck off, that was the next best thing. Still, I hoped she could read my thoughts. I hoped she could see what her son had cost me—cost us all. If she believed I hadn't done the right thing after all that?

Well, then she was complicit—which made her worse than her son in my book.

Just in case she could read me, I made sure to remember each and every atrocity I'd witnessed that had a direct tie to Lucifer. Each murder, each torture, each chess move that brought about so much pain and suffering. I willed it to her mind, hoping she would see, hoping she was the mother I thought she was. Despair hit her expression—a loss so great it showed on her ancient face.

"I see," she whispered, her tone defeated before she turned her full attention to her son. "I will accept Cronus as the last sacrifice. The Blood Moon bargain is complete."

Gaia reached out, caressing her son's face for one long moment, her eyes studying him as if she would never see him again. Tears gathered in her eyes for a moment before they spilled down her face. In that next instant, a black web of magic bloomed on Lucifer's cheek where she had touched him. His mouth opened in a scream of agony, and as bad as the thought might make me, I was glad I'd turned off his voice.

Lucifer's skin began to die, the flesh necrotizing in

quick time, spreading out down his neck and across his face. He fell to his knees, the blackness snaking down his arms and torso. He brought his hands up just as his fingertips began to crumble to ash, his body quickly following suit.

It happened so quickly, my brain couldn't process it. So soon was he snuffed out that my mind and body were still waiting for a villain in the wings to come out and kill us all.

Gaia wailed for the loss of her son, but as soon as Dušan wrapped her up in a hug, she quieted. He whispered in her ear words none of us could hear, and I hoped she was comforted. I didn't envy her in this, and even though I knew she did what was right, I still felt an echo of her pain.

Gaia swallowed hard and pushed Dušan away before striding over to our huddled group. She stopped right in front of me, her pale-blue eyes assessing me for a long moment. "My complacency and omissions have injured you and yours. For that, I will give you a gift of my choosing. It is too difficult a task to ask you to choose your own gift, and I would not ask it of you. Instead, my gift will be given freely. In addition to that gift, and although you may not want it, my previous offer stands. I will tell you all the things you do not know. I will impart my wisdom to you in the hopes that you will be better than me. I refuse to be your enemy, daughter of Chaos, and I hope, one day, you can forgive me."

I accept. And... I'm sorry for your loss.

"And that's why you're already a better goddess than I ever was," she answered my unspoken thought. With that cryptic statement, she raised her hand and snapped her fingers.

Nothing happened at first, but then a light bloomed in the formerly dark gate which had shrunk to the size of a door in our inattention. Despite Gaia's insistence that she was giving me a gift, I had a tough time believing that anything good could come out of the realm Lucifer had made. I actually flinched when the doors cracked open. Even Alistair's arms tightened around me—either in answer to my flinch or for protection.

A man with a head of white hair strode through the gate first, his face more haggard than what I'd seen in the previous times we'd interacted. Rowan Durant looked like he'd been put through the wringer, and as fun as that was to see, it wasn't what I'd call a gift.

That was until I saw who he was holding hands with.

Two women walked with him, both dark haired, both beloved, and both lost to me. In his right hand, he clutched Lilith's hand, and in his other...

I fell to my knees in the dirt, unable to handle the unexpected joy that punched me in the gut.

Maria.

And then I was up, sprinting across the crevasse to meet her. I probably wasn't the only one, but I was getting to her first. The stupid dress hindered my steps, but I yanked it up and kept on running. It was completely possible I may have accidentally tackled my sister to the dirt, but the way a laugh peeled up her throat, I didn't think she minded.

"I can't believe it. I can't believe it. Fates, Ria." I squeezed the shit out of her, clutching her to me like she could be taken away at any moment.

"I'm okay, Max. I'm okay. Everything's okay," Maria cooed, rubbing my back like she was comforting a child.

It was then that I realized I was sobbing, but I couldn't give a single shit. My sister. I had her back. Dušan said she was gone, so I never thought it would be possible to have this. To see her again. To have her in my arms.

Maria giggled, and I pulled back to stare at her face. "Are you really you? Do you remember what happened? Tell me something only Maria would know."

Please don't let this be a trick. I don't think I'll be able to handle it if this isn't real.

She smiled at me then, the gentle curl to her lips as mischievous as my Maria always was. "Yes, I remember what happened. I stuck that bastard like the pig he was, and then fell for a really long time. I remember everything,

Max. Everything. Like when we were kids, you would occasionally slip an inordinate amount of dandelion in our mother's tea to turn her stomach."

I snorted out a laugh and then winced, hoping Teresa didn't hear that. "Okay, I believe you."

"No need to thank us, Max," a voice called—one I had not expected to hear in this place.

I glanced up from my and Maria's roll in the dirt to see Ian in full-battle regalia smiling at the pair of us. He looked different here in Faerie, his once-dark-brown eyes blazed bright, their amber cast telling of his death-goddess heritage. He stood next to Rowan, who I had a feeling was not who he appeared to be, either.

"Everyone in this damn place has two names," I griped. "So I figure you're what? Hermes, Thanatos, one of their kids? What?" A staff appeared out of nowhere in Rowan's hand, the two serpents and spread wings a dead giveaway. "Hermes it is then," I muttered.

It really did make a ton of sense—especially the trickster nature and air abilities. Plus, he always seemed to be at the right place at the right time.

Rowan's hangdog expression lifted, and he gave me an elaborate bow. "At your service, Max. I must say, you did a sight bit better than I thought you would."

I only nodded. Rowan was the king of backhanded compliments, and I refused to rise to the bait.

Not today.

Not when I'd gotten such a gift.

"Don't antagonize her, Hermes, she's had a trying day," Lilith scolded, and I couldn't help it, I laughed.

I got up, dusted myself off and pulled Maria with me, dragging her to Lilith as I gave her a one-armed hug. I had a feeling I wasn't going to let Maria go anytime soon. Lilith's arms closed around me, the zing of her power racing across my skin, letting me know she wasn't just a figment of my imagination.

I wanted to ask how they were back. I wanted to know everything.

But they were back, and safe, and alive.

And it could wait.

CHAPTER TWENTY-SIX

"Maxima Christina Alcado, if you don't get out here right this second, you are going to miss it!" my mother called, fit to be tied. I had to say something about my mother, it didn't matter if I was a goddess or not, she was still my mom and wasn't going to let me get away with squat.

Especially when we had a schedule to keep.

I didn't have a good reason for stalling, but here I was, trying to calm down and failing miserably. Nerves rose in my gut, the same ones that had been plaguing me all damn day. And the previous night. And the week.

Warm arms closed around me from behind, one banding around my shoulders and the other my belly. Without even opening my eyes I tilted my head back, resting it on Alistair's shoulder.

"You're doing the right thing, love. You were so confident a week ago, don't let your need to fix everything ruin it for you."

Alistair was right, of course, but all I could do was smile as I remembered the expression on my birth father's face when I told him and Lilith in no uncertain terms that I was retired, and they could take the crown they wanted to saddle me with and shove it where the sun didn't shine.

After the reunions in the crevasse, Gaia bestowed amnesty to the trees, letting them live with her in the deep fissure in the earth. Since it meant that they didn't have to die, and they were mostly peaceful, they had no problems with the arrangement. After that mess was done, Gaia returned to her tree, leaving Lucifer's ashes to blow in the wind. I had a feeling she would be grieving his loss a lot longer than she would ever let on.

Dušan took that opportunity to whisk us back to the Seelie Court castle where there was food and wine and more conversation than I really wanted, but I didn't quibble. The only one of us who got out of the revelry entirely was Zillah who was still unconscious. I'd started to worry about him, but Dušan informed me that he hadn't slept a single minute since Lucifer was remanded to his cage, and he was taking a well-deserved nap.

During our feast, I'd caught Lilith and Dušan talking about what I would do with the crown, and what changes

I would make to the Seelie Court, and I fucking lost it on the both of them.

Lilith, I understood. She had no idea how much I did not like being an authority figure, nor did she have a single inkling of the conversation I'd already had with Dušan in his little pocket world. About how I didn't want to stay here in Faerie—no matter how beautiful it was. About how I had a family and life back home, and I wanted to live it.

Even with as much that had transpired since that talk, I wasn't going back on it.

"You should know better," I scolded my birth father, the creator of worlds and gods, one of the most supreme beings in the whole universe.

Yeah, I said what I said.

"You know good and damn well I'm not a Queen, and I never will be. *You know.* As of this very moment, I am retired," I announced, standing with my hands planted on the table, staring down my birth father and adoptive grandmother. I also may have knocked over my chair in my haste to stand up, but that was neither here nor there. "I will not be Queen. I will not be Sentinel. I will not be anything. As soon as I can, I'm going home. Do you two hear me? *Home.*"

Dušan's lips stretched into the most mischievous of smiles, the little sneak. "I know, daughter. We just wanted to see how soon you would announce this. We figured a little push wouldn't hurt. It's time for you to start living for you, my beloved daughter."

When would those two ever learn to quit with the maneuverings and just ask me about shit? I considered how old they were. Likely never, would be my guess.

Many drinks and much food were consumed, and when we reached the ends of our energy, we all paired off and went to sleep. I did notice—even though I'd kept her to myself for the majority of the night—Maria peeling off from the group to go with Ian at the end of the night. He'd been occupied by his overprotective brother for most of the evening, so I didn't feel too bad about stealing her away.

I was just glad they were together finally.

Over the coming days, I learned how Ian and Rowan broke into Hell, rescuing Lilith and Maria from the Seam. Well, it was more like Ian—with his new knowledge of who his mother was—went on a hair-brained adventure which most certainly could have gotten him killed, met up with Hermes in Hell, caused mayhem and mischief, but also managed to get the job done. Hermes had been sent by Gaia to retrieve my sister, her gift set in stone before I ever took a step into the Unseelie Court.

That particular story scared about a century off my life, and ended with me socking Ian and Rowan in their respective arms before hugging them until they couldn't breathe. Yeah, I was grateful, but dammit those two were idiots.

But the rescue itself was more than two-fold. Lilith had known when she went up against Lucifer that she would die. Blessed at a very young age with the ability of foresight, she knew just how she would lose her life, her die cast long before I was ever born. She also knew when she did die, she wouldn't go to Heaven or Hell, but the Seam —or rather Tartarus—where all gods go in death. Lilith also knew that if she managed to find Maria, she would pull her from that place if she ever discovered a way out.

The other major thing that came about was Dušan's decision to retake his throne. I was happy to abdicate my position, but rules dictated that there be an event so the Fae could accept their new ruler.

The Fae were sticklers for rules, after all.

So here I was, in a very pretty dress, getting ready for my father to retake the Seelie throne. I couldn't say for certain why I was nervous. Maybe it was because I was still waiting for the other shoe to drop. I'd had a lot of joy in such a short amount of time, my natural inclination was not to trust it.

Hadn't that been the way my whole life? My mother and Della and Lilith were working with me on this—Lilith especially since she reminded me that every time the shoe dropped it was because Lucifer himself had done the dropping. Now that he was no more, there would be very little in the way of major catastrophes in my life for a while.

We hoped.

"Come on, love," Alistair whispered in my ear, "The sooner this is done, the sooner we get to go home and lock ourselves in the house for a good long while. I figure doing my part to help save the realms from Lucifer should buy me at least a month of vacation."

I spun in his arms, rising up on my toes to meet his lips with mine. "Maybe two."

By the time we heard a throat clearing in the doorway, my lipstick was a mess and so was Alistair's face. Whoops. Around my husband, I should definitely always have on smudge-proof lipstick. I snapped my fingers to right us before letting my gaze fall to the door. Della and Aidan were in their Faerie finest, likely coming to collect us because my mother had zero intention of walking in on Alistair and I. Again.

"Honestly, you guys," Della huffed good-naturedly, "It's like you're newlyweds or something."

"Yeah. And when you're on your honeymoon, you can jump each other's bones as much as you want, but until then, we've got a job to do," Aidan griped, pulling at the collar of his shirt, grumpy as ever. I was going to need to find him a girl.

Later, though.

Della and Aidan, along with Hideyo had decided to stay on as my paladins—refusing to renege on the promise they made to Lilith. Della, however, would stay in Faerie, watching over me when I came to visit, while Hideyo and Aidan stayed on the Earth realm. I was going to miss Della being around all the time, but with the newly installed Fae door in her Tandrirr home, we could see each other anytime we wanted without the freaky trip through the trippy fog-filled forest.

It wouldn't be the same, but I was so happy for her. She'd missed her family while staying with me. I was glad she could go back to them.

"We're coming." Alistair sighed, his hand tightening over mine as we swept from the room, ready to begin our lives together.

The Faerie event brought us all manner of creatures in my father's retinue. The elves from Tandrirr, the dwarves and fawns. Even the pixies and water Fae made an appearance, and the party moved outdoors to one of the many pools of water so they could be comfortable. A few of the sentient trees—which one of the fawn called Gnarus—managed to come to the party, too. I was glad they were being included.

A vast majority of the Fae were happy with how the monarchy had shaken out, and Dušan's re-coronation went off without a hitch. Many of the Fae were glad someone like me—an outsider—was giving up the crown. I could tell they were wary, especially after Verena, but most remembered life under Dušan's rule and the prosperity that was found during that time. I was delighted that they would have that back. Well, that, and the fact that it wouldn't be me dealing with the headache it would be to fix all the shit Verena trashed under her rule.

I was slow dancing with Alistair, so freaking happy I could burst when Andras tapped on Alistair's shoulder.

"Mind if I cut in?" he asked, and I pressed a kiss to Alistair's lips before going to my father.

It was weird that I thought of both Andras and Dušan as my fathers. Neither had been with me for the majority of my life. But knowing what each had sacrificed, what the pair of them had gone through to keep me safe, I figured they both deserved the title of Dad. Plus, I supposed it was like any other adopted kid or stepparent situation. I had two Dads, a mother that had sacrificed everything to keep me safe, and a grandmother that was as badass as they came.

It was more than some people got, and I'd take it as the gift it was.

"Are you happy, Max?" he asked, a faint thread of worry in his expression.

My smile had to be radiant as I answered him, "Yes. More than happy. More than anything."

He nodded before taking me through a turn. "Do you think your mother would want to stay with me? Even with my new position, I mean?"

The vulnerability on Andras' face made me pause. Lilith and Hades had decided to co-rule Hell, which had been their purpose and position before everything went pear-shaped. Now that Lilith no longer had a husband to oppose it, and Andras was no longer in exile, she restored him as a Prince of Hell.

And Andras wanted to know if my mother would stay with him? After four hundred years without him, I had a feeling my mother would be with him in a heartbeat.

"Have you asked her?"

Andras shook his head, a blush rising on his cheeks. "What if she says no?"

"She's not going to say no, Dad. Mom loves you. She's always loved you. Even when you were being a secret-keeping, manipulative dick. Just ask her. Ya'll will work it out. I'm sure of it."

Andras smirked at my dick comment, his dubious smile stretching to a grin when he caught sight of my mother dancing with Striker. The pair whirled toward us, and we switched partners in a move that was so smooth it had to have been a spell. I let my mother have it and settled in with Striker.

I hadn't spoken to the man much since we'd returned,

me too busy with coronation shenanigans and him too busy with his reunion with Melody. He was learning what it meant to be a father to a succubus infant and a real partner to someone. All of which was probably blissful for a man like Striker as much as it was trying. I had a feeling Ronan would be a big brother sooner rather than later, and that made me so fucking happy I could burst.

"You going home still, right?" he asked as he led me through a turn, his tone apprehensive.

If he meant Denver, then the answer was yes. Alistair had no qualms about making Denver our home base—especially after he found out how much NOLA grated on me. "That's the plan. After some time off, I'll head back to the shop, too. I really miss the old place."

My fingers actually ached to hold a tattoo machine again.

"Do you think..." He trailed off, took a breath, and tried again. "Do you think I could come back? Melody would like to go home to Denver, and I really would, too. Now that she's no longer getting mind-bended by Verena, she has no desire to stay. We don't know which line her family is from, and there isn't really a need to find out. I think we'd all like to get back to..." He paused again, leaving his thought dangling in the breeze.

"Normal?" I offered.

"Yeah."

I thought about it for maybe a millisecond. "I think I'd like that."

INSTEAD OF STAYING ANOTHER NIGHT IN FAERIE, after the party—that had to have lasted at least two days, I didn't give a shit what the sun and moon said—we traveled to Tandrirr to test out the newly built Fae door. The door—my first—led to a room in my basement adjacent to the casting room. I'd put more than a few protections on the thing, as did Dušan and Hermes. I had a tough time trusting Hermes—especially since he was considered a trickster by many—but since I'd found out who he really was, he'd become way less of a dick.

Especially after I gave him a hug and said thank you. I had a feeling not many gave him credit for helping us. I'd never be able to repay my gratitude for bringing Maria back to me.

Never.

I'd never been so glad to see my basement in my life. Exhausted, Alistair and I trekked up the stairs, heading to bed. Tomorrow—or whenever Maria and Ian came up for air—we'd meet for brunch or dinner.

We had time. Lots of it.

That's all I'd ever really wanted—time with the people

I loved. And now we had an infinite amount of days ahead of us.

Together.

THE END

This concludes the Rogue Ethereal Series.
It has been an absolute pleasure sharing Max with you.

Please keep reading for a sneak peek at my upcoming projects.

DEAD TO ME
Grave Talker Book One

Seeing dead people and solving their murders is Darby Adler's bread and butter.

What's not on the menu? A nosy Fed poking around her crime scenes who seems to know a hell of a lot more than he's saying--especially about the ghosts surrounding Darby and the murderer who's desperate for her attention.

-Preorder now on Amazon-
Coming September 29, 2020

NIGHT WATCH
Soul Reader Book One

Waking up at the foot of your own grave is no picnic...
especially when you can't remember how you got there.
Cursed with powers she can't name, Sloane Cabot has
vowed to catch the Rogue who turned her into a monster
and killed her family. Too bad a broodingly hot mage is
bound to keep her on the straight and narrow.
Whether she likes it or not...

-Preorder now on Amazon-
Coming November 17, 2020

THE PHOENIX RISING SERIES

an adult paranormal romance series by Annie Anderson

Heaven, Hell, and everything in between. Fall into the realm of Phoenixes and Wraiths who guard the gates of the beyond. That is, if they can survive that long...

Living forever isn't all it's cracked up to be.

Check out the Phoenix Rising Series today!

ARE YOU A MEMBER OF THE LEGION YET?

To stay up to date on all things Annie Anderson, get exclusive access to ARCs & giveaways, and be a member of a fun, positive, drama-free space, join The Legion!

facebook.com/groups/ThePhoenixLegion

facebook.com/AuthorAnnieAnderson

twitter.com/AnnieAnde

instagram.com/AnnieAnde

amazon.com/author/annieande

bookbub.com/authors/annie-anderson

goodreads.com/AnnieAnde

pinterest.com/annieande

Printed in Great Britain
by Amazon

44050515R00166